FIGHT FOR HONOR

Written By

Elina Salajeva

Created By

Elinadeivid

DISCLAIMER

This is a work of fiction. Names, characters, businesses, places, events, and incidents are either the products of the author's imagination or used in a fictitious manner. Any resemblance to actual persons, living or dead, or actual events is purely coincidental.

DEDICATION

To all people who believe in something, people who understand and strongly believe that in life we must stand for something, and be able to fight to protect our interests, our way of life, to defend our freedom and safeguard our rights.

Touchladybirdlucky Studios

A David Gomadza Production.

Elina Salajeva, Elinadeivid have asserted their rights under Copyright, Designs and Patents Act 1988 to be identified as the author of this work.

ISBN: 978-1-9164397-4-0

[Touchladybirdlucky Studios]

ISBN: 978-1539716792

[Createspace]

ACKNOWLEDGMENTS

Many thanks and best wishes to the Elinadeivid brand. Big thanks also to Touchladybirdlucky Studios.

CHAPTER ONE

"In life we all have something we stand for, something we strongly believe in, this is the purpose of life. At least we all must fight for something. And when our freedom and rights are threatened, are we not to defend that at any cost? What's the price of freedom? What is the price of our rights? Rights to make our own decisions, to choose what we want in life? When our way of life is threatened by one man's greedy to conquer and dominate the world are we not to fight? Are we not supposed to fight for honor? Are we not supposed to stand and defend ourselves? Our kids? Our way of life and to defend our survival? When one man's greediness threatens our way of life, are we not supposed to fight for honor? Every day new rules are imposed, and our freedom is restricted. We no longer have a say in things that matter to us. Every day our brothers and sisters are persecuted. Our way of life is under attack Are we not supposed to fight? Our leaders vanish with no trace and now we cannot say anything without being considered as enemies. All we want to do is to defend what's rightfully ours."

After the massacre of thousands of innocent civilians by the then government there was a new world order. Things had changed. People no longer trusted their governments. People had voiced their concerns. They had fought for the establishment of a third-party to oversee the security and protection of people. Governments had become so oppressive that there were considered as unfit for the purpose. The majority had entrusted third parties with the task of providing security and protection. Third parties who were answerable to the people and the government as well. Or so the people thought. It was not until after two years had passed that the people suddenly realized that they had traded one devil, for a worse devil. The private third-party establishment now responsible for security and protection had seen an opportunity to control everyone themselves and imposed harsh rules and regulations. The government had lost control of security and protection. No one was safe. A greedier and ruthless man was now the head of security and protection. He wanted to dominate the world. To control everyone. To impose rules where you either obey or perish. This man was hungry for power and control and no one would stand in his way. Many had vanished without a trace and many had been murdered in broad day light. It seems no one and nothing, was going to stop this man. Can one woman's discipline, commitment and dedication stand in the way of this man. Can she fight for honor and save humanity?

Tanya was a highly committed and dedicated young

lady. She was brought up in a family of two children. She had been brought up in a family with strict parents. Having had her father spent some years in the presidential guard regiment. Discipline, honor and true to oneself was preached to her since she was a kid. She had had great grades in school and came out as one of the best in her class. By now, she could speak five different languages, Latvian her native language, Russian, Polish, English and Germany. She was highly committed to whatever she did. After leaving school she had joined the presidential guards regiment. To fulfill her dream of protecting the President and other high-ranking officers. She had spent years in training preparing for a life which she had wanted since she was a kid. She spent years training at the regiment of the federal services with the status of a special unit. This regiment had the responsibility of protecting the President and other state officials. The regiment was also responsible for maintaining a guard of honor at selected high-ranking places. After three years of training, she had finally qualified as a presidential guard and left the regiment to start working for the President. A few years after working as a presidential guard, things changed. The world order changed as we know it today. The riots had resulted in the massacre of many innocent people. People had voted for the nomination of a third-party that was to be endorsed with the responsibility of security and protection. This meant a complete change of power from government to third parties. The third-party was an independent establishment, and this establishment was now responsible for all kinds of protection. They were now responsible for security and protection of the

President, responsible for law and order, responsible for guarding banks, treasures and high-ranking officials. This was a total shift of power from the government to an independent establishment. This meant a shift from working for the government to working for this independent establishment. The independent establishment had strict vetting and enrolment rules that seems to prohibit some. Those guards and security personnel who were employed by the government and who were responsible or involved in the massacre of many people the days of the riots were often turned down for jobs by the new establishment now responsible for security and protection. This saw Tanya among those turned down to protect the president. They had offered her a job if she complied with their demands, but she had vehemently refused as she saw this as a betrayal of her beliefs and things she stood for. All her life she had dedicated everything to protecting the president and now it was hard to do what she loved. Her dream had been shattered, the new establishment had requested a security vetting and a medical screening and imposed so many conditions which she saw as infringing her freedom and her rights. After the death of many activists, Tanya decided to establish a private investigating company. She started to investigate the deaths of all well-known people, former activist, former security officers, former presidential guards and other opposition personnel. She had noticed a pattern developing. These deaths were all somehow related. All the people who had died were at one-point had worked for the new security and protection establishment or either they were vehemently opposed to this establishment. That raised suspicion and fear to some extent as she had vehemently opposed the new establishment as well. Will she be able to do her investigations without coming into conflict with whoever was behind the murders? Will she end up dead like everyone else who had opposed the new establishment. Deep down these are the questions that kept coming to her mind. She knew, the new establishment had a part in the deaths of all these people but could not prove it. She remembered all those years in the regiment, training to protect and serve and to fight for honor. Letting this devil go unchecked was against all the things she stood for. She knew somehow; she had to do something; she had to find a way of proving that this new establishing was equally bad as the previous government if not worse. The new establishment was responsible for the deaths of many directly or indirectly. She had found it difficult to collect information and evidence as she was not in the security and protection system. She had refused the vetting and medical required by the establishment and this meant that she had no authorized excess to any files or information or any dealing with those in the security and protection whatsoever.

CHAPTER TWO

Juliet had spent hours researching about the new company she wanted to join but there was nothing suspicious about the company. It seemed that it was clean; the government had approved the company, and it was part of the security and protection which had become a global brand. She arranged an appointment with Brian to meet for lunch and discuss this further, which they did before meeting Brian's boss. They later spoke to Brian's boss, and he also explained that there was nothing to be afraid of. The vetting was simple and straight forward, they looked at your history and involvement and whether you were linked to any riots groups, and if you are a threat, then, what level are you, will there be able to offer you a job or not? In other words, will you be a risk to the security and protection program? He went on to explain that the medical involved a thirty-minute procedure just to check your blood and marrow for genetic disorders and diseases that might affect you in the future. This was purely for insurance purposes as you were employed by the security and protection program who had their subsidiaries who offered medical and life insurance and they required all this information to cover that. And as an employee of the security and protection program they were responsible also for your health and wellbeing. It made sense, and she agreed. They scheduled an appointment. Patrick had not seen the professor for a week. He had started developing feelings for the professor. Going for a week without seeing her had driven him mad. He counted on seeing her over the weekend as she had told him that she didn't work weekends. Weekend passed by and no sign of the professor. On Sunday Patrick broke into the professor's apartment, he was afraid that something bad might have befallen her. But she was not there as the place was protected and part of the security service as soon as he broke in, an alarm was sent to the headquarters and the security services responded swiftly. He was corned quickly and taken for interrogation. He explained that he was worried about the professor; they questioned him about his relationship with the professor, and what he wanted from the professor. He insisted that she knew him, and she was helping him and since nothing was stolen and apart from the damage to the door after a phone call to their boss they let him go out on Sunday evening. Sunday evening the professor finished work and went home. She had never worked continuously like that before. She felt very exhausted, all she wanted was to go home and have a long bath, a glass of wine and a good night sleep. Day of the procedure arrived for Juliet and she went for the security vetting process first which took two hours to complete.

They collected a lot of information about her. Her finger prints, her iris scans and a body search among other things. The medical, lasted forty-five minutes. It involved completing the consent form. Then questions took fifteen minutes to answer and the actual procedure around thirty minutes. After the procedure she went home and looked forward to start working for the same company as Brian.

She had spent the past two years grieving for Frank; it has been a hard road but at last she might be able to move on. She had looked to spend some good time with Frank but that was not meant to be. Even if she was partly to blame, all she did was in good faith. She wanted things to be perfect. She was to start work after two weeks from the day of the procedure. They spoke with Brian for several hours over the phone. They were friends and Frank brought them together. After the death of his friend Brian had at least wanted to help his friend's girlfriend. He had failed to find out what had happened to his friend at least all he can do is help her adjust. And finding her a job at the same company as him, brought some sense of resolve over the issue. Brian's university girlfriend Melissa was pregnant, she was his wife now and over the coming weeks after getting his job saw Brian spending less time at home. He started spending less time with his wife and spending more hours at work. His wife trusted him, so she had nothing to worry about until he started spending more time over the phone talking to Kristian. Brian's wife had met Juliet, since applying for a job at the same company as him, Juliet started phoning him any time to ask questions and discuss the job. It was nearly two weeks after the day of the vetting process and the medical that Juliet received a phone call from the company he had applied a job with. They phoned to confirm she had passed the vetting process they had checked her past and medical and they were looking forward to meeting up with her anytime soon and looking forward to seeing her at work after a few days. It was great news; it meant a pay increase three-fold that she was getting at her old company. She received the phone call on a Friday afternoon and she was going to start work the following Monday. For the first-time since the death of Frank, she found the need to celebrate and move on. In her heart she will always remember Frank. She phoned Brian, but he was not home and left a message as his mobile phone was out of reach. That evening she tried calling Brian again but this time he was available they spoke for hours. She looked forward to going to work the next Monday. After talking to Brian, she invited her friends including Mary. They had a celebrating party that weekend. Brian had come back from work that Friday to find his pregnant wife sleeping, and it was just after 7pm. She had never slept so early before.

"Darling, why are you sleeping this time? Are you ok?" he asked as he entered their bedroom.

"Nothing darling, just feeling tired probably it's to do with this pregnancy," she replied as she got up out of the bed. He changed his clothes, and they all went downstairs in the lounge. Brian's wife Melissa had listened to the message left by Juliet but had deleted the message. Although she trusted her husband he had changed, he used to rush home to her, he used to be sweet, he would kiss her all the time, he would buy gifts more often but now he had stopped doing all that. After work he would come back home change and phone, Juliet. She didn't suspect anything or stopped trusting him, no, it's the divided attention which started annoying her. She was pregnant with his baby and now he seemed like he had lost interest. If not on the phone he would be on his laptop sometimes until early in the morning. She started sleeping early when he is not home, she started feeling lonely she knew he loved her, but I guess she just wanted all the attention women crave for especially when they are pregnant.

CHAPTER THREE

Just a week after Juliet's medical, the position she applied for was finally declared as no longer available. The position was there since the day he got his job. It seemed like the job was meant for Juliet. That week he came across his old friend Daniel the one who had told him about Calvin's death. Daniel had met Calvin just before the day he died, and they had spoken for some time. Daniel had expressed concerns that Calvin was saying some people were trying to kill him. Calvin had hinted that he was refused work from the same company Brian was working for because he refused to undergo the medical. He had accused the owners as trying to kill him. He remembered that he himself had chosen to have the medical. Ok, he thought to himself anything suspicious about the medical? He started researching about the medical but could not find anything wrong with this, it was a well-known procedure in all medical books. He started to research about his company. The days he researched just days before he got the job, there was not any bad publicity. The company was part of a global network owned by the gazillionaire called JT, but he was as clean as a whistle he, protected presidents and ministers. Professor Anya after work went straight home, by 7 pm she was home, and JT had informed her that her apartment was broken into by a thief and can be repaired the same night or the following day. The professor knew who had broken into her apartment and she realized that it was safe to play it down otherwise they will start snooping around. Patrick was a perfect subject for her experiments. After spending time with that miracle baby, she had believed that human testing was safe and did not want to raise suspicion. She went home and waited for an hour just in case Patrick visited her. Her plan was to take a long bath and a glass of wine and sleep until tomorrow. She didn't want to wake up. 8pm still there was no sign of Patrick so she decided to take a long bath. She took a wine glass and a bottle of wine and went in the bathroom. She went into the tub and sipped wine and relaxed in the tub. At 8pm Patrick was released from the security and protection headquarters. He had his background checked and had his prints taken and his photo taken. He had refused but was told that to be released he was to give these as a condition of release. He wanted to see the professor badly, so he finally admitted and 8pm he was out. He left the headquarters and headed straight to the professor's apartment. The bedroom light was on as he arrived, she was home, and he was very happy, he didn't even knock at the door, he just opened the door through the broken glass on the door and went inside. He went straight to the bedroom, but she was not there he went downstairs and saw that the light in the bathroom was on.

"Professor, professor!" he shouted trying to open the door, but the door was locked. He knew she was inside as the door could only be locked from inside. He knocked the door but there was no answer.

"Professor, professor! Are you ok?" he screamed banging the door. He knew something was not ok. He started banging the door louder and louder. The neighbors heard the noise and called the security and protection service. It took him about five minutes to finally break the door and he just couldn't believe what he saw.

She lay in the tub face down, quickly he rushed to her aide, but it was too late. He tried lifting her up, but all her skin fell off, it was horrendous, he looked in sheer disbelief. The woman he wanted was dead, in such a manner he could not explain, all his life he had never come across something like that. Literally she was cooked, all her skin was coming off, all his hands had her skin stuck on them. He felt disoriented he knelt next to her, he touched the water, but it wasn't that hot. So, what had happened? He realized that this was more than what it seemed, he got up quickly and decided to run. It took a few minutes to go downstairs and outside the apartment, and as the door closed behind him he felt a sharp pain in his head and a warm feeling of warm water running down his face. And that was the last thing he remembered.

CHAPTER FOUR

JT was in his limousine when the phone rung, it was an authoritative voice on the other hand, short precise and to the point.

"Sir, target taken, both cleaned, over and out," JT listened for a few seconds more, but the phone line soon died. He held the phone for a while, he put the other end of the receiver on his chin before putting the receiver in its place in the limousine. On the other side of the town, Juliet was very happy and had looked forward to starting work on Monday. She had had celebrated the job with Mary and other friends, it was great she felt good about everything, at last it was time to move on. She had grieved for Frank and this was a new chapter in her life.

Sunday night she decided to take a bath just before she slept, she put on her favorite CD by Carolinadeivid: Angels and Hot lips, she took a glass of wine and entered the tube. She had been through a lot and finally she was going to start a new life first with a new job. She sipped wine and listened to the music. She picked up the phone which she had placed next to her and dialed Brian's number but there was no reply. She lay in the tub for a few minutes before starting to dose. Another five more minutes she thought to herself this was it at last it was time to move on. She had sacrificed relationships all the university years and the last two years since Frank's death were unbearable. She stood up and left the bath tub. Suddenly she found it hard to breath, she dropped the wine glass on the floor shattering it into pieces. She felt temperature rising so fast that she felt like she was being cooked from inside out. She rushed to the bathroom basin cutting herself on the feet in the process from the broken glasses on the floor. She drank water quickly before she started feeling dizzy. She felt like someone was choking her. She couldn't explain what was going on if she had had the chance she wanted to phone Brian and ask him for help, but everything happened so fast that all her organs started shutting down. Slowly she still could hear Celine Dion's song fading away, and that was the last thing she heard. JT was still in his limousine when the phone rang again. He picked up the receiver and listened.

"Subject two out. Over," and there was silence and this time he put the phone down quickly and puffed his cigar. All the people who had left his bunker team, all died in mysterious ways. Anyone he didn't trust be it government ministers or not perished too. It was Monday morning, and it was like any other day, business as usual. Brian had looked forward to meeting Juliet that day. He was expecting to see her as soon as she had been inducted and shown her office and from his experience that will be roughly an hour after the start time.

He carried on with his work as normal until after one hour when he tried to call Juliet to find how well she was settling on. There was no answer, he thought that maybe she was still being inducted so to try again after another half an hour. After half an hour still there was no reply her phone kept ringing. It was not until coffee break at 10am when he decided to go and see if she was in her new office. He knocked the door, but her office was locked, and lights switched off. It seemed like no one was even there the whole morning to his surprise. He went to his managers' office to ask. The manger informed him that she had rung in stating that she was unable to take the job. On hearing this Brian was shocked, it contradicted everything he knew, he remembered talking to Juliet, she had expressed interest without doubt and the excitement of starting the job. He had never felt so confused in his life, something had happened. He had not reacted quickly when Frank, his friend disappeared. This time he was going to do something quickly about it. He phoned again to find out the whereabouts of Juliet. Still there was no answer. He ran to his car and drove to Juliet's place. He had let his friend down before; this time he was going to do his best. A lot of questions kept running through his head, was Juliet okay, why did she not turn up for work, if the manager is correct why she not told him. He checked his calls list, yes, she had tried to ring him but did not leave any message. Maybe she had gone to his place maybe he should tell his pregnant wife that he had left work, and he was going to Juliet's. He rang Melissa, but there was no answer. Where is she he thought to himself? It was only after 10am, maybe she was still in bed or downstairs. He tried the house phone but still there was no reply. He decided to leave the message. Melissa heard the phone ringing, but she was in the bathroom. Brian had left a message asking her to meet him at Juliet's house something bad might have happened.

CHAPTER FIVE

She changed quickly and drove to Juliet's. Brian tried ringing Juliet's phone again but still there was no answer. As he left the city heading towards Juliet's house he started feeling very uncomfortable. His temperature rose suddenly, he found it hard to breath and concentrate. His vision was blurred.
The car started swerving from one side to another. His organs started to shut down. He felt like being cooked from inside it was very painful that he was in and out of unconsciousness. His car hit the side of the bridge and fell into the river. A few minutes later he had been cooked to death. Brian's wife Melissa arrived at Juliet's house she phoned Juliet's phone, but it was ringing but there was no answer. She phoned her husband, but the phone was switched off. She broke Juliet's house door and rushed inside. She saw the bathroom light on and rushed there first. She pushed the door open and was horrified by what she saw. She stood at the door for some seconds in

shock. She was lying there on the floor bleeding. Was she dead or not? Fear crippled her and after a few seconds she found courage and rushed inside the bathroom to check if Juliet was still alive. She stepped on broken glass and slipped, and she fell hitting her head on the corner of the tub. As she fell she came face to face with Juliet whose eyes where open like those of a dead fish. She looked like she has been cooked. She tried to scream, but she had no energy left in her. Slowly she felt feeling sleepy and warm blood ran down her forehead and the last person she remembers was Brian. Meanwhile many miles away from the city a young man in his mid-twenties is being buried. A large crowd of mourners has gathered. It's a wind day with dark clouds covering the sky, it's a little cold and it seems the heavens were mourning too for the loss of such a bright young man. Birds could be heard singing in trees surrounding the cemetery. It seems as if saying last goodbyes to the young man whose life has been brought to an abrupt stop unexpectedly and so hurting that most of the crowd who had gathered had never met this young man. It's the pain for such a loss that unities humans that brings humanity together. Most of the mourners had heard the sad story about his death on television, radio and through newspapers. They had been touched and saddened by the sad story of his death especially the manner in which he had died. His death was such a shock that it did send shock waves all over the country. There were similar deaths before in several cities, but they haven't been highlighted as much as this young man's death had been. When the young and bright start dying unexplained deaths, it brings a chilling cold shiver through the spine of all human beings. They were people of all ages, the young as well as the old. A very large crowd had gathered and spread all over the cemetery. It felt like it was the death of a well-known liked leader of some sort, yet this young man was hardly known. Most had no idea who he was, but it was the manner of his death that had brought people together and caused the uprising and riots which were still taking place in several cities. It was a very disturbing time for the family as they had waited several weeks before they managed to get his body for burial. There was a lot of bureaucracy involved, they were several delays in getting his body for burial. The authorities had objected to all the demands put forward by the family and relatives and the leaders of the opposition to have the body released to them early and be examined by the institution of their choosing to determine cause of death as they disagreed with the version they had been told. By the time they got the body for burial several weeks after his death they could not perform any rituals or examine the body as it was in a bad state. It seemed like a relief for the family as they finally put their loved one to rest after weeks of mourning and fighting for answers to no avail. His death and burial left many questions unanswered, they had struggled for weeks since they were first informed about his death, it seemed like an ever-going agenda and they seemed to get nowhere. An autopsy was denied or carried out in private, but they had not been informed about the real cause of death and a request to get the body for private tests had been denied despite the whole country being brought to a standstill by protests. The local medical institution had offered help with funeral and burial cost as an apology to the delay in releasing his body for burial. It had been several weeks since his death and his relatives, his family, and a lot of people most who hardly knew him had gathered at his parent's house. The funeral was held for several weeks and this had financially crippled his parents. This was their only son, they had used all their savings putting him through secondary school and university. They had hoped that one day this young son of theirs would have a brighter future and repay them all their savings and be able to look after them in old age. The pain of having their dream shuttered by his death was so unbearable that his mum tried to kill herself. Their only child had his life cut short and to make things worse he was in excellent health and the morning of his death he had talked about his plans to one day buy them a very big house and he had promised to look after his parents in their old age. His father was heartbroken even worse, he had sat his son down and had had a father to son chat about life and whom to trust. His father strongly believed that his son's death had not been an accident or suicidal as the officials later suggested. This had caused a rift between himself and his wife. The father had strongly denied help with funeral and burial costs from the medical institution, he had seen such an act as a betrayal of his trust, his son and everything he had stood up for especially after the refusal to release his body early for burial. After his death and burial, the parents grew apart and finally separated months after his death. The wife moved out of the family house and went to stay with her relatives in a different city. The father started drinking since his wife moved out of the family house and since the loss of his son. His son was in his final year at the university and they had worked hard all their life raising their son and giving him the best education, he can get. The couple had been very unfortunate as their first-born daughter died as an infant and after the son was born the mother learned that she was unable to have any more kids at the advice of doctors as she had a difficult birth. Since the day they learnt that they were never going to have another child, they cherished their son and promised each other to give him the best life they can. They had separated when their daughter had died suddenly, and they had not believed that it was possible for a healthy infant to just die few weeks after birth. They were rumors that the father had blamed his wife on drunken occasions that maybe she had accidentally suffocated the baby whilst they both slept together. The mother had vehemently denied that and pleaded innocent to such accusations. It had been a hard time for both and several months after they had split up they patched up moved in together and tried for another baby and God responded swiftly as months after getting back together they were blessed with a beautiful boy. And it was only after his birth that they learnt that this was going to be their only child. This baby had brought them very close together it cemented their relationship, and they cherished every day they spent together. For those who knew them when they heard that their son had died and that they had split up, it was not a surprise as they knew that their son was the cornerstone of their marriage and sole purpose of their existence. Such a loss was unbearable to them, and it was hard for them to try to comprehend why their kids had died first instead of them. It was just not the norm of things, they had had several stories of kids looking after their parents and grandparents in old age. Both had lived to see their parents and grandparents grow old and wrinkly and die in their old age. Losing a kid was hard enough, and they didn't understand what wrong doing they had done to be punished by God that way.

CHAPTER SIX

Frank was a very handsome young man full of dreams and ambitions, in his young age he had realized that his parents were the best in the world, they loved him very much. They had both worked very hard throughout the years raising him. He considered himself very fortunate after learning that his sister had died when she was an infant and especially learning also that their parents were unable to have another baby since his birth. He had done very well in school and university, he valued life very much as he always wondered what it would have been like if his elder sister hadn't died as an infant. Growing up as a lone child had modeled him, several nights alone in his room he had wondered what life would be like if he had had a chance to have a sister or brother. All his friends had brothers and sisters and some many enough to fill a small minibus. He had valued family ever since his growing up and one day he had promised himself to have a large family of his own.

Frank was such a bright student that he won several prizes and had admiration of several lecturers and students and a large following of female admirers. He was 74inches high and of well-built body. He was very handsome with a broad face and strong chin bones and an infectious smile. He was a well-built man and regularly visited the gym to keep himself fit. He had a very strong voice, and he easily had the attention of the people. He was one of the determined and ambitious people you will ever meet. He was once in the rugby team in his first-year at the university and had not played any major sports after his first-year. He spent most of his time on academic stuff and research. He had had one serious relationship in his first two years at the university which ended when his then girlfriend Angela got pregnant and aborted the baby to his distaste. He was gutted and didn't agree with the killing of his baby as someone who had been an only child this baby had meant a lot to him. But on the other hand, his girlfriend had been unrepentant about the abortion, the baby was going to ruin her career as she puts it. It meant taking a year off university to give birth and look after the baby. Probably if it wasn't for her mum Angela might have kept the baby because she loved Frank and this baby would have meant a lot to both of them especially knowing that Frank was a lone child. But when her mum discovered that she was pregnant she disagreed and strongly recommended abortion. Angela's mum had dropped out of university herself when she got pregnant, planning to give birth and return to finish her studies of which after birth she found out that it was hard. After the abortion Frank split up with his then girlfriend Angela and decided not to have any serious relationship until after he had finished his studies. He had only one year left, he decided to put his head down and try to achieve his dreams. At the university he had several friends, he was such a charmer that he found it easy to get friends, and he got along well with everyone. He had at least two people he thought he can call friends, people he can trust and tell secrets. Denis was doing a different degree program at the university to him. They had met in the gym it seemed they didn't have a lot in common apart from their interests in befriending iron bars. They spent their time together in the gym or restaurant sometimes in the university play grounds exercising in the open air. Calvin was short but of a strong body build, he had a round face and a golden tooth that shines every time he smiled. He had lost his real tooth during his first-year at the university. He had fallen prey to the first-year pranks at the university and found himself in a brawl which resulted in the loss of his front tooth. That first-year brawl had built the man he was today. He had spent several hours in the gym since his first- year. As he remembered it when he first arrived at the university he was a short skinny guy easily picked up on, he remembered being pushed around and being bullied and after that brawl he had made an oath that he would do whatever it takes to stay in shape. He had grown so fast and big to become a very strong man. But it was hard for him to find friends as some abstained from him. The only friend he had known in his first-year at the university had accused him of misusing steroids and no one could explain the sudden growth in size since the university brawl, but he had put it all down to hard work in the gym. He worked hard in the gym and had won the admiration of Frank and ever since he confessed he was an only child the two had become inseparable for some time. If it wasn't for this, they could not have been friends because apart from that they had no common interests. They were doing different degree programs. Calvin was more of a desperado when it comes to women, Frank on the other had was a ladies' man he turned down offers of dates from the university female students. Calvin was somewhat a shy person he rarely attended gatherings at the university whilst Frank was a leader and, on some occasions, had played a big part in gatherings. He was a natural leader, he commanded the respect of students and professors alike. He had a big voice a large face with a big chin bones that made him look serious whenever he spoke. He had a smile that made him be liked even by his enemies had he had some. It seemed he had no problems at all, he was always happy whereas Calvin was strong but a moody person. Growing up alone had meant that sometimes he just wanted to be alone. On several occasions Frank had gone to his university studio flat to find him locking himself in the flat. He had gone to the gym on some occasions when he didn't want to just to keep Calvin company. Deep down it felt like he had found the brother he had never had. He had always imagined what it would be like growing up with a brother. Frank had his fears as well, but he never showed or talked about it, his parents were his major fear. They had sacrificed all their savings to give him the best education and life he can possibly have. It was a big burden to have such responsibilities and expectations from his parents. He had worked hard to do well at the university. He had promised to repay his parents their dedication and love they had shown him by buying them a huge house and looking after them until old age. He knew it would take time and hard work to fulfill his promise to his parents. He had taken out a student's loans for his research and his parents didn't know about this. The death of his sister as an infant had left so many unanswered questions and the fact that they couldn't have kids after his birth only worsened the situation. The death of his sister had always nagged him. Was it mum's fault as the rumors had it? Was it a natural infant death? If yes was it genetic? If genetic is it hereditary? Are my kids going to die young too? Might I die young too? What are my parents thinking, can they survive the loss of another child let alone an only child? These are the questions that kept ringing in his heard. Brian was of medium built but a handsome tall guy with a face that seemed to say what you see is what you get. He had been brought up in a very strict household. He was a straight-talking person known to be ruthless in his judgment and as cold as a snake that kills for fun. He had no crocodile tendencies of shading deceitful tears. He was like a hungry hound when he says he's going to bite you he will do it in a flash before you even blinked. He was such a ferocious and ruthless guy that most girls at the university never thought he had or was brought up by a mother. His father was at some point, a long time ago in the special unit of the military that protects the City. His memories of his father were faint since he had died when he was a little boy. He had been brought up by his grandfather who was also of military background. They had shared a flat at the university and that's how they met. Despite his strict character they had a lot in common apart from the fact that he had several sisters and brothers. They heated it off well since their first-year at the university and ever since had become very good friends. Frank felt that Brian was his real friend a real mutual friend unlike his friendship with Calvin which was more of a brotherly nature. Brian was more of a friend than a brother, they talked about anything. The only activity they didn't do together was going to the gym. Brian didn't like spending too much time in the gym he preferred spending a lot of time with his girlfriend rather than romancing iron bars. They normally had no secrets, they shared same flat in their first-year at the university and ever since had lived nearby each other and see each other most of the time. They were doing the same degree program and seemed to have same goals and ambitions. Brian didn't value big families having been brought up in a large family. His childhood memories were scrambling, quarreling and fighting for food and use of facilities with his brothers and sisters. He had confessed that he was going to have just one kid, this was one of their source of arguments with Frank. They all seemed to come up with very compelling arguments for and against big families and at the end fail to agree.

CHAPTER SEVEN

Frank pressed the button and waited for the lifts, few more people gathered behind him, all whom seemed occupied by their personal worries to be bothered to take notice of other people. A female voice can be heard coming from the speakers above the walls touching the ceilings. Frank looked left and right there seemed to be very different people minding their business. Several questions seemed to keep on coming to his head, his heart was beating a bit faster than normal. He took a leaflet from his pocket looked at it and put it back in his pocket. Is this the right thing to do now? Can I start worrying about this now or wait until I have handed my dissertation?

"It's a lovely day today?" said a woman standing beside Frank. There was a bit of silence.

"Sorry, are you talking to me?"

Frank asked looking around and at the lady standing next to him. Frank didn't even wait for the lady to reply him before he added.

" I hope it stays this way the whole day," the lady smiled and continued.

" Fingers crossed, but it's a shame we are stuck in here we should be out there enjoying the sun."

"Ah, you work here? I am just visiting eh...," Frank didn't even finish before the lift doors opened. He put his hand in his pocket and took out a small piece of paper, he looked at it, folded it and put it back in his pocket and went into the lift. The other people followed including the lady he was talking to. He looked at her and she smiled, he checked his time before running his fingers down his chins and giving a sigh of relief. His heart was racing very fast, people came and went in the lift and Frank seemed not to notice until a female voice can be heard saying,

"Level 7 Doors opening". He looked around and found that the lady he talked to was still in the lift.

"Take care bye," he said whilst coming out of the lift and looking at the big directional sign in front of him. He followed the directional arrows to a double glass door that opened instantly as he approached. In front of him was a very big reception and several seats on the opposite side with people seated. The weather was humid; the air conditioner can be heard rattling trying to keep the air in this reception cool. A lady in her late thirties is seated with her head down writing something down. She had dark hair and wearing reading glasses, she seemed exhausted from the hot weather as Frank approached she lifted her head and with what seemed to appear as a leaflet she blew cold air in front of her face. She looked at the air conditioning fans above and shook her head.

"How can I help you?" she asked Frank as he approached.

"I just realized that I am an hour early, I have an appointment at 2pm," she looked down as if reading from an appointment list in front of her.

"Ok, Mr. Frank take a seat we will call you when your turn comes. Next Please!" shouted the lady.

Meanwhile miles away the sound of the fire alarm can be heard, but no one seemed to panic or take notice. Everyone seemed to be very busy with whatever they are doing. A bell can be heard, and the lift door suddenly opened and a lady in black came out running towards the corridor as if reacting to the fire alarm.

" Sir, Sir," she shouted.

She ran a few steps forward in high heels, she had her hair tied upwards, and she was wearing glasses. She had a white overall coat on top and she was holding a file in her left-hand. She was in her late twenties or early thirties.

"Sir, bad news again," she paused catching her breath, she seemed a little distraught she handed the man in front of her the file she was holding and with the right hand she removed her glasses and wiped her eyes with the two fingers of her left-hand.

"I am afraid it's a failure again. We have lost the subject, we tried everything we can to bring him back Sir," she looked upwards and closed her eyes and took a big breath.

"With all the resources I provided you with are you telling me you can't get this project going?" remarked the man in a dark suit who was walking in the corridor with what appeared to be his bodyguards.

He stopped and took off his sunglasses, he looked at the file, looked at the young lady and said.

"I want the full report on my desk tomorrow morning

and I want to see you in my office when I get back."
He put on his sunglasses and marched out of the building, he left the lady stood there with a file in her hand. She stood still and watched him march out of the building. Back in the building where she was working, the young lady approached one of the man in a white overall coat and said.
"Listen the boss want the report by tomorrow morning so tell me what's the problem. How can we keep losing our subjects? What's wrong professor?"
These two had worked together for a while now. They were part of the team selected to work on this project some few years back. Since its launch the project was a failure. This had caused most team members to spend most of their time in the lab. Professor Tango was a well-known physicist; he was a fan of Albert Einstein. He had spent all his career trying to apply Albert Einstein's quantum theory $e=mc2$ to the benefit of human beings. Instead of using this formula for destruction he tried to apply this theory to the good and superiority of human kind with the help of the well-known world recognized biologist. He had seen an opportunity to use Albert's theory of relativity of energy and human metabolism to the benefit of mankind. His theory was based on the assumption that at any given time all things being equal, energy or body activities can be exponentially increased, and this was to help soldiers in war times, sports personnel and those with chronic illness. Over the past years the test in the lab and on animals had proved a success but human trials had ended in disaster. His theory was based on the notion called the copycat effect. Professor Tango proposed that at any given time other things being equal the body's

energy levels and metabolic activity will match or copy and exponentially increase in quantity or activity to match that from an external source if the optimal or breaking point levels are introduced into the body system. For instance, professor Tango proposed that any increase in energy levels from an external source like an energy drink will result in the body's energy production metabolism matching that from an energy drink and exponentially multiplying this at the optimal level breaking saturation point. He proposed that the body will copycat or match and or exponentially increase the external source levels if the optimal level is supplied into the system. If less or more external source levels are supplied the body won't match or copy the external source levels but will try to make use of the supplied levels. If the correct optimal levels are supplied, the body will produce similar or exponentially multiply the levels. Taking energy levels for example, a banana with 100kilojoules of energy if eaten by a human being and the optimal levels to trigger a reaction are near 100 kilojoules the body will copy or match these energy levels and or exponentially multiply the energy levels. The resultant energy levels will be 200kj or greater as the body copies or matches supplied energy levels of 100kj. On the other hand if a body needs 100kj to initiate an exponential reaction but the energy source has less than 100kj let's say 80kj or more than 100kj let's say 120kj the body will not react but only utilize what has been provided in its system. This discovery has led to amazing results in the lab, tests on mice were successful. They had managed to exponentially increase energy levels as long as they supplied correct levels needed to initiate a reaction. Test in monkeys were successful but tests in baboons which are better representative test subjects to humans were inconclusive. There was no reaction, no matching or copying of energy levels. It seemed the baboons simply utilized the supplied energy levels without themselves matching or copying the external source levels. Despite his disagreement tests on human beings had begun with detrimental effects. There was a lot of bureaucracy that proper protocol was not followed or just pushed through not based on tests results. A lot of personal intimidation was directed at the professor; at one-point he had quit only to be dragged back to the Lab from his home in the middle of the night.

CHAPTER EIGHT

The local gazillionaire businessman JT had seen the enormous benefits to be gained from such a project that he had injected some of his money into this project. Beyond professor Tango's views the local businessman had seen absolute power, and he knew that this project was going to make him not only the richest man in the world but the most powerful and feared man on earth. The gazillionaire businessman had companies all over the world he had companies manufacturing weapons for the army and police in the form of guns, laser guns, Taser guns, software and intelligence. He had companies supplying satellite services. He had spent several $ billions and years trying to develop the ultimate weapon to no success until now. Over the past year's unknown to anyone else the gazillionaire had manufactured over 100billion small silicon chips enough for every human being and big animals. Unknown to anyone apart from his underground team. His dream was one day to rule the world, at one-point he considered himself to be God that's how big this project was to him. Over the years he had realized what the professor and his team had missed over the years. His experience in the army and in dealing in weapons had made his dream come true and tests on human subjects had begun to no one's knowledge but himself and the underground bunker team. The following morning the gazillionaire was driven by his chauffer to his office in a big limousine. The car was very long, and it seem to take priority on the road, the limousine was of a red color with a black nose. It shined, and the morning sun seemed to caress its metal body giving it a nice shiny color. The limousine had tinted bullet and fire proof glasses, in his early years he had survived an assassination attempt and that lead him to wear a bulletproof vest. He still had a scar on his chin from a metal shrapnel from the last attempt. He had discovered that it was easy to be killed by a cheap assassin over a stupid argument and for nothing, leaving his billions. His phone kept ringing and his secretary was taking messages as they went to his office. One of the callers was professor Anya who phoned to confirm that she was going to meet the gazillionaire in his office that very morning. In his office JT is seated on a very comfort chair with his legs on the table swinging from side to side puffing a big cigar. He looked at the ceiling whilst puffing his cigar before a female voice can be heard saying the professor was here to see you. JT asked his secretary Clara to let the professor in, and just as he had finished talking on the telephone system a knock can be heard on the door. JT puffed his cigar again and asked the professor to come in. A large door beautifully decorated opened, and a smartly dressed young looking lady came in holding files. She walked forward towards the large table. The office was a very big office with very beautiful engraved decorations. It appeared to be twice the size of the normal office. There were two seats in front of the table. There were huge picture frames with photos of JT so big they looked like movie posters. The office had a huge oval second glass door facing the beautiful view. JT stood up still puffing his cigar and walked towards the windows, he opened the window and stood near the oval glass door looking at the beautiful view.

"Eh professor what seems to be the problem?" remarked JT putting off his cigar and walking towards his chair.

"It has been three to four years now professor? And it seems this project is not going anywhere. I have invested a lot of time and money professor," he stood up again and walked towards the oval glass door. He looked outside again and walked towards the professor who was still standing there with a file in her hand? He told the professor to sit down as he took the file from her. He briefly looked at the file and sat on the corner of his table facing the professor. "Professor, I need results and not excuses! Do you know what this will mean to the world out there? Do you know the great things I will be able to accomplish? This will revolutionize and forever change life as we know it today. Imagine how this will revolutionize medicine as we know it, how this will revolutionize sports and how this will change for example period it will take to give birth? Just imagine not having to wait for nine months to give birth? How about that?" He leaned forward to the professor before continuing.

"Just imagine giving birth after only three months, imagine giving birth to a healthy baby after only three months?"

He stood up and walked to his chair and sat down putting his legs on the table and waited for the professor to talk.

"On all subjects there is no reaction, we seem not to identify the trigger or how to induce the chemical reaction," she paused for a while before continuing.

"The only time we nearly had a reaction the subject suffered some form of metamorphosis` with catastrophic consequences."

"We need more time, we decided from next week to look at this from a different angle and hopefully this time we can give you great results," added the professor.

JT removed his legs from the table and sat up straight and looked into the eyes of the professor, for a minute or so silence broke out. The professor knew something was wrong by the look of JT's face. She leaned forward and put her hands on her knees and waited for JT to talk.

"I have bad news for you," he paused a bit and continued.

"I am going to terminate the project in a few weeks' time so start cleaning up, I would have loved this to continue professor," JT stood up and walked towards the oval glass door.

The professor sat there speechless, she removed her spectacles wiped her eyes and tried to talk JT in keeping the project. She tried her best to persuade JT, but JT had made this decision some months ago. To him it was not a financial reason for ending the project, he had excellent news from his underground team they had made a breakthrough. Ever since, the professor and her team were now a problem. The professor had objected vehemently to the idea of human testing without satisfactory results on animal testing. Ever since the breakthrough, JT had let the professor continue with the project as a sudden end to the project could have raised suspicion, and that's the last thing he needed. The professor was a little too honest to the dislike of JT. He knew to be successful and dominate one had to break or ignore rules at some point. The only way now was to get rid of the professor and her team. He knew success was in keeping these away, he didn't want them snooping around. JT assured the professor that herself and her team were to be paid in full. After 8 weeks the project was closed. The professor had worked hard spending countless hours in the lab with her team. She had been employed by JT whilst still at the university. She had spent her university years researching on ways to manipulate the natural human metabolic system to increase energy levels, to fight diseases and speed up reactions without any side effects. This was going to revolutionize life as we know it today. This was going to mean a big step for human kind this was to be a manipulation of human metabolism to speed up everything like healing processes and growth functions. JT had the same vision but to him it was more about making people superhuman by manipulating and exponentially speeding up everything in a controlled manner. He had spent most of his young years in the military. He had wanted to produce a super human being too fast, too strong, a human being who can heal in minutes if wounded. He had seen having such a power as to the ultimate requirement to be the king of the world. The professor was gutted when the project was terminated, she still believed a breakthrough was still in their sight, but they had no funding.

CHAPTER NINE

Frank had been sat at the reception for about an hour, people had come and gone. Inside seemed even hotter than outside, the air condition didn't seem to work. It was humid; he had stood up several times to drink water at the reception. He looked at his watch stood up and went to the toilet. After using the toilet, he looked in the mirror and washed his face with cold tape water. He took some hand drying paper and dosed his face. He went back to take his seat, and it was now 13:45pm. As soon as he had sat down, he heard his name being called in the speakers which were above the ceiling. The female voice repeated his name and informed him to go to room 2 and wait for his appointment at 2pm. He stood up and walked towards rooms with numbers above them, he knocked room two door and entered the room. There was a lady sat in the chair typing something on the keyboard. As he entered, she asked him to seat down. He sat down and started looking around the room whilst the woman was typing something down. She raised her head and greeted Frank and introduced herself to him. She put her hand on the mouse and said.

"Wait let me bring up your file," she looked at the computer screen and scrolled down using the mouse.

"Ok, what seems to be the problem?" she looked at Frank and rested her back in her chair waiting for Frank to talk.

Frank explained his situation, he wanted to make sure there were no any genetic hereditary problems with him. His elder sister had died as a young infant and his previous girlfriend had aborted his baby and as an only child he wanted to rule out any genetic disorders. Although his girlfriend had seen a baby as an obstacle to her career, he had not believed that was the main reason she had aborted the baby. So many questions kept coming to his head. Probably his girlfriend had suspected that he had a hereditary genetic problem or was it because his sister had died weeks after birth that she aborted his baby. He never expected her to abort their baby, he had hoped that she would keep and conceive his baby. Meeting Juliet a few weeks back had driven him to book this appointment. She had shown interest in him and had hinted on starting a family with him whenever he was ready. Him having been brought up as an only child, Frank wanted to have a family early in life. After realizing the mistake, he had made of rushing things with his ex-girlfriend Angela. He had researched the procedure on the internet before going. If everything genetic wise was ok, he had promised himself to start a serious relationship with Juliet, the lady he had met a few weeks back. He explained what he wanted to find out, and the doctor explained what he had to do to get his blood genetically screened. It was a very simple procedure as the doctor explained. The procedure would be used to extract a part of his bone marrow to screen for any genetic hereditary problems or any abnormalities with his genes.

"This is a simple procedure that lasts about 15-30 minutes, it is simple and fast, a small hole will be drilled on your hip bone to extract the marrow, and the marrow will be taken and sent for screening," she paused and started typing something on the computer. She stopped typing for a while and looked at Frank.

"There will be a local anesthetic and you will be wide awake," she paused and murmured something as she continued typing.

She opened a drawer and took a leaflet and some forms, she ticked some parts on the forms and crossed some before handing the form to Frank.

"Mr. Frank look at these forms they explain the procedure in detail, take them home think about it and give me a call if you are ready to have it done so I can book you an appointment," she signed one of the forms and gave all to Frank.

"Don't eat six hours before the operation and everything should be fine," she put down her pen and looked at Frank and asked if Frank had any questions. He looked at the leaflets for a few minutes, he murmured to himself as he read through the leaflets.

"Oh Yes, one thing!" he looked at the doctor and put the leaflets down.

" What are the side effects of the procedure and how long it takes before I get the results?" he rests his back against his chair and waited for the doctor to respond.

"No side effects this is quite a simple procedure, 15-30 minutes at most the procedure is done, only thing you can experience is a bit of pain at the site of operation and a little of numbness due to the local anesthetic which will last for a few hours or days and after that everything will be normal," she sat back and paused for a while, she typed on the keyboard and looked at the computer screen before talking to Frank.

"Yes, about the results, they take a week to two max, once I get the results I will let my secretary phone you and arrange an appointment for the results," she paused and looked at Frank.

"We have many people going for this procedure as the leaflet explains its simple and straight forward," she took another leaflet from her drawer and looked at it.

"Read the leaflets then let me know which day I can book you an appointment with the consultant," she sat with her back rested on the backrest support of the chair.

Frank read the leaflets again and after that he told the doctor that he was going to read and research more about the procedure and then arrange an appointment. He didn't stand up straight away, he sunk his head in the leaflets before standing up and thanking the doctor. As he stood up, she asked him to get all the telephone numbers needed from her secretary at the desk. 2:45pm he saw the time at the reception's desk digital clock as he left doctor Maurice's office. Three days after the appointment with doctor Maurice he telephoned her secretary to book in an appointment for the bone marrow extraction.

"Friday afternoon at 2pm, is that ok with you?" the secretary asked and waited for his reply. He did not answer straight away but instead seemed to repeat what she had said.

"Friday afternoon 2pm eh....," he repeated after her in a small voice.

"Oh yes! Friday is fine," he spoke into the telephone and waited for the secretary to confirm booking.

"Ok Mr. Frank the appointment has been booked," there was a pause and the flickering of pages can be heard.

Frank wrote down on a small piece of paper, Friday 2pm Doctor Maurice and put the paper in his trousers pocket. Juliet was a tall beautiful blonde lady with blue eyes and a lovely smile. She was one year older than Frank. They had met a few weeks before, she had graduated a year before and a had a good job with one of the leading financial companies. She had studied finance and economics at university at degree and master levels, respectively. She was a bright student, she had waited to raise a family until after university and after she had secured a good job of which she had done. Meeting Frank the other day was like a wish come true. She had found a good partner if not a future husband in Frank. She had everything she wished for, a good job, a car and had a beautiful house and the only thing that was missing was Frank. She remembered all those years at the university having to postpone serious relationships due to her studies. All those nights alone, the countless hours spent in the library and in her university studio flat studying instead of enjoying the best life has to offer, all that was a thing of the past. As soon as she met with Frank, she had hinted to him about him moving in with her. She had everything, and even better Frank was her dream man, he was handsome, fit and a real charmer. He was a good listener and a year younger than herself. What was not to like? She was ready to start a family if she met the correct guy, and it seemed she did, or she thought. She had two younger sisters, and all had kids, and this was the perfect time for her to start a family. Back at the university Frank is talking with Brian.

"What are you doing on Friday?" asked Brian.

"You mean this Friday? Let's see, ah... I am busy this Friday, oh by the way that reminds me to tell you this," he paused for a while.

"I met this lady a few weeks ago, I didn't expect it to get to this point," he stopped and looked at his friend. He touched his right-hand shoulder and his face showed real excitement.

"I think she might be the one," his friend was a bit surprised.

"How long have you known this lady, you sound like you been going out for some time?" they had always talked about everything and lately Brian had noticed some unusual behavior.

Frank had been keeping himself to himself and had been secretive lately. He couldn't believe his best friend had met a lady and not tell him. Looking at his friend's face Frank realized Brian was a little worried as he didn't show enthusiasm. He hugged his friend and tried to explain.

"My friend look, I didn't want to say things because I didn't expect it to come to this," he continued.

"We met a few weeks before, I think we hit it off straight away, but we were both kind of busy," he sat down on the edge of the sofa and looked at his friend.

"She rang me yesterday and asked if we can meet on Friday. She has a good job, a car, her own house, and she is really gorgeous man, I tell you," he smiled and looked away for a while before continuing.

"I had wanted a relationship after University, but it just happened and deep down I think this is my lady," Brian remembered seeing his friend that happy those days he was going out with Angela.

He was happy; he had thought he had found his dream lady in Angela only to be gutted after she killed his baby. He noticed that his friend was serious about this lady. He was happy for his friend, they talked about Juliet and their future after university. They talked for hours like they used to do.

CHAPTER TEN

JT is down in his bunker with his research team, he had been summoned down there as the news of a breakthrough had been received. The research had been going on for a few months now. This was started whilst the other project was in operation headed by professor Anya, JT had discovered what was needed to initiate a reaction. He remembered his years in the military. Professor Anya and her team had worked very hard to come up with the formula to identify and match needed optimum energy or body metabolism activity levels. There was no doubt on that part the project was a success but on its own it was not good enough. The real money and power was in finding a way to create that fusion that metamorphosis and induce the reaction. Hence the underground bunker researchers and scientists. He had secretly gathered the best scientist and academics from all over the world to take over from professor Anya. JT had used his experience and vast military knowledge and guided the bunker research team with astonishing results. He had suggested through an analysis of the jelly fish having experimented with Taser guns with his friend whilst in the military. They had used different Taser voltage to see at what levels one can be zapped to be incapacitated. They were surprised that at certain levels Taser voltage was beneficial as they seemed to gain more energy and aggressiveness when certain amounts were passed through the body. This had fascinated him as at one-point after being zapped at a certain voltage he gained more energy. He remembered having unexplained energies that he defeated his then opponent. Although at one-point he nearly suffered a seizure after being zapped. He knew that one day he would try to manipulate this to his advantage. After his experience in the military he had been fascinated by the jelly fish, when he heard about professor Anya's research many years ago, he didn't hesitate to invest his money in her research. His dream was way above that of the professor. The professor wanted the research to be used to help humanity whereas JT wanted a way to control human beings and a way to rule the world. He had seen how this could have been used as a powerful weapon. The underground bunker team had understood JT unlike professor Anya who was too honest to cut corners. The bunker team understood that they had to sacrifice humans to save humans. The research was going well but not as fast as they wanted. The jellyfish was somehow the key to the breakthrough, thought JT. Probably some external instant current was the catalyst or trigger for the metabolic reaction thought JT. The task or key was to harness such powers in the human body just as in the jellyfish. The jellyfish can carry such a current emitting organ without electrocuting itself and matching that in humans was probably the key to the success of this project suggested JT. He had bought professor Anya's ideas but went further developing this idea using his military experience. The professor was right but short sighted as she never looked at nature for answers. He knew the jellyfish was the key and had secretly funded projects to try to imitate a jellyfish in humans. If any reaction was to be induced like in the jellyfish an internal current emitting organ had to be present. Having discovered this, he had realized and invested in satellite and telecommunication heavily. He had paid loads of money acquiring satellite and telecommunication businesses and the chip industries. To him he had a plan, he knew that being in power was not far away from him one day he might rule the world. In the underground banker the team is gathered outside the glass room with a baboon inside. The animal seemed unconcerned as it takes a rest. They are all together talking and as soon as the lift metal doors opened and as they saw JT they started clapping hands. There are cheers and whistling that seemed to catch the attention of the animal in the glass rectangle the size of an ordinary kitchen that made the animal stood up and started pacing up and down. JT stood just outside the doors of the lifts for a while with his bodyguards surrounding him.

" It's okay," said JT as he started moving down the steps towards the scientists.

His bodyguards knew what he meant by its okay that

all went back into the lift leaving JT with the scientists. The lift can be heard going up as the noise made by the pulley system can be heard too. As he walked down the steps, the cheers become louder and louder more to the surprise of the baboon that it started making noises as well.

"We have a breakthrough! We did it!" he didn't even finish talking before they all started clapping hands and rejoicing.

The one who seemed to be the leader of the scientists approached forward to meet JT as he walked towards them. They all followed him quickly talking to one another. The leader of the scientist met JT and shook his hand excitedly. JT put his hand on his shoulder and congratulated him before the other scientist surrounded them. The leader of the group was known as Professor Clark; they had been working hard for the past few months. He spoke very fast to JT with a great deal of excitement.

"Do you want to see this," he said whilst raising his hand to one of the scientist as a signal. He didn't even wait for JT to reply he started moving towards a big computer station with state-of-the-art technology.

"Come please," he said to JT as he started moving fast towards the station. Once at the station, he raised his hand again and shouted.

"Professor please," the other scientist walked towards the glass box where the animal was. He typed something on the computer panel outside the glass box. He pushed some buttons outside the glass box and headed where the rest were standing. As soon as he started walking towards the others, the mechanical noise is heard, and some form or mattresses started rising from the ground surrounding the glass walls.

The animal became afraid and started running from one side to another making noises. Professor Clark was talking to JT at the same time pressing buttons on the computer keyboard. A loud female voice from the speakers above interrupted the conversations.

"Base parameters. Checked. Sealing and locking the Doors. Checked. Initiating the program. Countdown."

Professor Clark kept typing whilst the others waited eagerly talking to one another.

In the glass box form or mattresses surrounded the glass walls up to the ceiling. The glass box was as big as a large kitchen. Extra lights in the glass box came on and the animal looked confused and afraid as red flashing lights were switched on.

"Are you ready Mr. JT?" remarked the professor with a raised voice.

"Ok, ok, silence please we don't want to frighten the animal even more," said the professor as he pressed the enter button on the panel. There was complete silence, and some gas started filling the glass box making the animal nervous and hyperactive as it started moving from one end to another. After around five minutes the gas seemed to have all been absorbed by the baboon as the glass box became clearer again. The animal can be seen pacing up and down making howling noises.

"Begin Countdown. 10, 9, 8, 7......," a female voice can be heard coming from the speakers.

The professor handed JT what looked like a computer tablet and looked at JT for a while before saying.

"Enter Sir! Press Enter when you are ready Sir!" JT looked at the computer tablet for a moment, put one of his right-hand fingers on the tablet screen and looked at the glass box.

".3.2.1 Ready," the female voice can be heard from the speakers. Everyone stood in front rows all looking at the glass box, JT at one-point couldn't feel his finger on the computer tablet that he had to look at the tablet to make sure he was going to press the correct button. He was so excited and couldn't believe he was to realize his dream earlier than thought. He had waited for this moment for a very long time, a lot of nice thoughts were running through his mind. One day I will rule the world he thought to himself.

CHAPTER ELEVEN

Frank had waited for the appointment eagerly on Friday after the appointment he was meeting with Juliet the lady he had met a few weeks before. He was excited just wondering what life would be like with Juliet. She had hinted over the phone that she wanted to settle down and was looking for someone who was serious also to start a family together anytime soon. Frank understood that it was not rushing things, most people postponed serious relationships until after graduation. As soon as they have finished their education, it seemed like rushing things but on the other hand this will be the right thing to do or, so she thought. She was ready but was he ready as well? They had spent some time over the phone talking together. They seemed to be perfect for each other and Frank remembered the day they first met it seemed they were meant to be. They had hit it off straight away, but they knew they had no time to commit as Frank was busy with his academic staff.

She was determined to have Frank that she surprised him that other day by ringing him and asking him out. Frank had liked her but just didn't put too much emphasize on the idea of a relationship with her. The week seemed to have flown past quickly Frank noticed it was Friday morning already and wondered what he had done for the past few days apart from thinking about this day, the appointment and meeting Juliet. The fact that she was a year older than him did not put him off to his friend's surprise, as he had never gone out with someone older than himself. He liked Juliet, she was different and her being older and already working was an advantage to him definite she was going to keep his baby, so he thought. She had a house I mean everything she wanted, and she was ready to be a mum and maybe his wife one day. He had no lectures on Fridays, they talked over the phone with Juliet confirming the appointment later in the afternoon. He seemed very excited about Juliet that that morning he started having second thoughts about going to the appointment. Was it necessary? Can this wait? If I don't do this now when am I going to do it? These are the questions that seemed to come to mind as he lay on the couch after talking to Juliet. He remembered the first-time he had met Angela; it was such a romantic time for him. He was feeling the same too with Juliet, he was disappointed when Angela had had an abortion. Could Juliet be the answer to that, will he finally find some form of comfort over this? All his previous relationships he had initiated the dating process whereas this time Juliet had shown real interest and made the first move. She was mature, and because of her, love seemed to be the only thing he wanted. Surely, he had to find a way to finish his studies and pass with flying colors and start a serious relationship with Juliet. He somehow had to find a way to juggle the two both at the same time. He picked up his mobile phone and typed something on the screen before putting the phone to his ear. He could hear the phone ringing on the other end and he waited for someone to answer. His father picked up the phone.

"Hello, hello, how is you?"

"I am very fine, thank you, how is mum?" replied Frank sitting up.

She is doing fine. When are you coming to see us?" asked Frank's father.

Frank hadn't visited his parents in over 3 months, he had been busy with Uni stuff. He felt a little guilty for not visiting and tried to make it up to his parents. He spoke to his father for a long time. His father and him had a one-to-one talk over the phone. He had reminded Frank that he was an only child and he should visit his parents more often as they get worried sometimes about him. He reminded Frank that they were both getting old and would be happy if he visited more often. His father had wished he had a grandson or granddaughter to keep them company. He had asked Frank if he was seeing someone. He had wished he had married soon even still at university he was not bothered. He wanted grandchildren. He talked about life in general and gave his son general advice on trust, relationship and loyalty to his parents.

"Can I talk to mum, is she nearby?" asked Frank after talking to his father.

"Just hold on," said his father.

He put his phone down and Frank could hear his

father shouting his mum. "Darling, your son is on the phone, come please," there was a moment of silence and he can hear his mum talking to his father as she entered the room. She picked up the phone.

"How are you, why are you not coming to see us? Do you have a girlfriend now? I want grandchildren you know. This house is empty now. I have no company; your father wanders away all the time. Where to I don't know," Frank didn't even have a chance to answer before her mum continued.

"We miss you, please come and see us as soon as possible. How is my daughter-in-law?" there was a moment of silence before Frank replied.

"Very sorry mum, I have been busy lately with all the Uni work. Don't worry I will get you a big house soon...," Frank didn't even finish before her mum interrupted.

"My son, it's not the house I want, no, its grandchildren. This house is too big for me now," he paused and waited for his mum to continue but she also waited for him to speak.

"Don't worry mum I met someone we will talk next time I visit let's see when eh...," he paused and looked at the calendar.

" Oh sorry, I can't promise when, but it will be soon mum. I promise," he assured his mum that he loved them very much and that he will fulfill his promise to them.

He talked a little about the lady, he had met and wished they have children sometime soon. He told his parents he was meeting Juliet a lady he had met a few weeks ago. Probably she was the one to provide grandchildren for his parents. They talked for hours before she said.

"Ok son now I will pass you to your father," she put the phone down and shouted her husband to come to the phone. He waited for some time before his father picked up the phone, they spoke for a few more minutes and said goodbyes. Frank promised to visit them soon before hanging up.

CHAPTER TWELVE

Meanwhile in the underground banker JT and the scientist had gathered to witness the revolutionary impact their research was going to have on life and all aspect of life. This was to be a corner stone to JT's success. A lot of questions were running in his mind, was this going to work for sure? How was this going to mean to the world? He had waited a long time for such an opportunity. He waited with the others and the professor looked at him and gave a gesture that it was time to press the button. JT seemed to take no notice of the professor. He couldn't believe that he was to rule the world much earlier than he had anticipated.

"Sir, Please. The button," remarked the professor looking at JT who seemed to be miles away.

"Oh sorry, here we go," said JT before pressing the start button. They all waited patiently, and it seemed like a long wait. Nothing happened for a few seconds. The baboon stopped and looked like it was sitting down. The baboon growled as if in pain looked upwards as if in pain and stretched its back before it seemed to disappear. Suddenly it was on the other side of the glass box. There were clapping of hands and loud applauses and this even unsettled the animal, and, in a flash, it moved from one corner to another. JT turned to look at the professor who applauded in excitement. JT hugged the professor and shook his hand strongly.

"You did it, you did it," remarked JT congratulating the professor and his team. "How is this going to last?" asked JT.

The professor kept silent for some time he looked at the computer screen in front of him before answering JT.

"This time only a few minutes, you see Sir! The dosage predicts the time the reaction will take and the intensity as well," JT looked at the glass box for a while before asking the professor about the side effects.

The professor explained that so far it was restlessness and complete shutdown for some time depending on the dosage. He assured JT that they were working hard to rectify the side effects. They watched in the bunker until the baboon stood still and fell asleep. The professor raised his arm and one of his team mates went to the glass box opened it and injected a sleeping agent into the blood stream of the baboon.

"We don't know what happens after this process, we are still in the gray area if you know what I mean," the professor looked at JT who in turn asked why the sleeping injection.

"Such super-activity, we believe might have damaging effects to vital organs if uncontrolled. After such an experience I think since it's new to the baboon's system the body will react to avoid further damage. In so doing shut most of the activities and body functions to sort of protect them from further damage if you know what I mean?" He paused for a while. He keyed in some figures in the monitor before continuing.

"You see this sleeping aid will help the baboon as this will fool its metabolism to think that the baboon is simply sleeping. In that way the vital organs won't be shut. To be honest, it's too early to tell what happens," this is the first-time we have successfully introduced the external energy sources and the baboon matching and exponentially exceeding these levels.

Last time the baboon came around after two hours. Hopefully we will expect him early because of the sleeping injection.

They waited patiently for the baboon to come around. Half an hour passed with no reaction at all. A further forty minutes passed and still nothing. Then after an hour the baboon first opened its eyes. Then stood up. Then after another twenty minutes it was up and running again.

"I think it took less time than the first-time for the baboon to come around because now the body has some form of memory. So, I think more tests, and this will be stored in the baboon's memory or metabolism. The more this happened the more quickly the body will adjust to this and after several times I think the shutting down will stop."

There were huge applauses when the baboon came around the professor explained that it was still in the early stages and more tests had to be performed to assess any damage to vital organs. He assured JT that he will do his best to solve the problem. He had noticed that JT wanted to move fast to human testing. After getting rid of professor Anya he saw no reason why they had to delay, she was the only possible threat to his plans. Now that she was no longer working for him nothing was destined to stop him. He had seen her more of a whistle blower. In a different city a young man in sprinting or what looks like cycling clothes has been brought to the A&E. Doctors and nurses are rushing the young man to the A&E's operating room. In the speakers above the wall a female voice can be heard calling doctor Newton to the A&E. Everyone is rushing around and shouting to each other, the young man is on a push bed being pushed by the ambulance services. A drip is attached to him, he looked unconscious and lay still on that push bed.

"Check for vital signs," shouted one nurse whilst retrieving the paperwork.

" What happened?" asked the hospital nurse as she took over from the ambulance crew.

"We had calls, found unconscious, cause unknown probably fell whilst cycling or running, no sign of a bicycle. Faint heartbeat, think suffered trauma. Body temp 40'C blood pressure...," after he finished the handover the hospital nurses rushed the young man to the operating room. The ambulance crew stood there for a while before going out of the hospital.

"We are losing him, people!" shouted one nurse.

"Oh no he is going into cardiac, where is the doctor," shouted the nurse as she injected something into the young man's blood stream.

The doctor rushed in and asked the nurse about vital

signs. They soon brought a machine with wires attached to it and attached all these to him. An oxygen mask was placed on his face. Everyone was rushing around and shout things to one another. A beeping sound can be heard coming from the machine.

"We are losing him," shouted one nurse and the other nurse came in with a machine whilst the other nurse cut the T-shirt he was wearing at mid chest level. Two things that appeared like small irons are drawn from the machine, brought in and the nurse holding these shouted.

"Clear!".

The other nurse moved away from the young man as the other nurse placed these small irons on his chest. Very fast she removed the iron from his chest and shouted clear again before placing these back on his chest. As the irons are placed on his chest, his body moved up and slumped back to the bed again. She repeated this one more time before a continuous noise can be heard and a straight line appeared on one of the machines he was attached to.

"We lost him," shouted one nurse and suddenly all of them stood around for a while looking at the young man's lifeless body.

One nurse took the file that was on his bed and took a pen out of her pocket and started writing something down. Cause of death unknown, JD, probably cyclist or jogger, probably hit and run, no major wounds apart from face bruising. Action; inform police. She closed the file as others came to take the body away. Before his death they were reports of a man acting strangely, eye witnesses referred to a man running at same speed as cars wearing same clothes as the deceased, but no one could confirm this. There was no bicycle that was found, and more surprising he had no any identification and had no major bruising to suggest a hit and run. The autopsy discovered that before he died his body's vital organs had shut down whilst still alive. His internal organs looked like they were half cooked. It seems he had experienced some high temperatures probably that forced his body to shut down to protect his vital organs. It seemed he falls unconscious and slumped to the ground. On examination it seemed he had two recent wounds at his back but surely not associated with his death or moments before his death. They appealed for help in the area he was found unconscious, but no one knew him.

CHAPTER THIRTEEN

After making the phone call to his parent's Frank started tidying up his apartment, he couldn't stop thinking about Juliet. He knew there was a chance that she might ask him to bring her back to his flat. He picked up small pieces of paper which he normally writes notes on from the carpet and took off all on the walls and his study table. He put all in the bin, tidy up the table and took all his clothes and put these in the washing basket ready to be washed. I will do all these on Saturday or probably take all these to Juliet's place. He stopped at this thought and smiled. Too soon he thought to himself, he went to the leaving room and took all clothes that were on the couch and stuffed all these into the laundry basket. He took all the cups and glasses into the kitchen and placed all these into the utensil washing machine. He put on a Robbie Williams CD and started listening to one of his songs. The song angel was being played and unconsciously hummed to this tune. That morning he had also phoned Juliet to find out if they can meet earlier than they had planned, he had thought of canceling the appointment and spend more time with Kristian. She had told him that she was busy that afternoon but would be free later and to meet as planned. Time seemed to have flown past very quickly, Frank looked at the time 12noon, and he started preparing for the appointment and he set off soon after 1pm. It was a very beautiful day; it wasn't very warm. There were clouds and a cool breeze moved the tree branches from side to side gently. It seemed like a relaxed day and for most people it was business as usual. There was traffic congestion and for some twenty odd minutes he was stuck in the traffic jam. He put in the Dreams, Money and Airplanes album and scrolled to track number 11. He waited for the track to start before the traffic started moving off. Angels with Hot Lips song was playing as he drove to the appointment. He saw it fitting that he had chosen this track. Juliet was on his mind whilst listening to this track. At last he reached his exit and left the motorway. He drove for another 10mins and he could see the building where he was going from a distance. He entered the building and went to the lifts, he entered the lift and pressed the level 2 buttons and the lifts door closed and the lift started going upwards.

" *Level 1,*" said a female voice as the lift stopped and the doors opens.

An old man came in and pressed the level 7 button. After one level the doors opened.

" Level 2," shouted a female voice.

Frank left the lift and started walking towards the reception in level 2. There was no one at the reception, he looked around and saw a self-serving point. Please check-in yourself for your appointment read the message on the screen. He typed his initials and a list of possible names came up. He scrolled down and selected his name. An automated voice is heard acknowledging his booking in and advised him where to seat. He didn't sit for long before a lady came asked for his ID and wrote something on the clipboard. She handed Frank some forms to complete before the procedure. He read the paperwork first, he noticed it was the same paperwork the doctor had shown him. He read until the bottom part, he looked at the lady as if asking for a pen, without saying anything she hands him the pen. He scribbled his signature on both copies and gave all to the lady. She read the paperwork and checked if he had signed all parts. She tore the back papers from both forms and gave them to Frank.

"We won't be long we will let you know when we are ready?" said the lady as she walked away from Frank.

He looked at the papers he had been given, they explained the procedure. He knew after a maximum of 30 minutes the procedure will be over, at one-point thought about the pain but remembered the doctor telling him that local anesthetic would be applied and that he will be awake. It wasn't the procedure he was concerned about, it's the results that he seemed to worry about, for some time he had forgotten about Juliet. He sat there for a few minutes more before that lady came back. She had a tray and asked Frank to put all his belonging in there, mobile phone, lighter, keys, coins, belt and wallet. He stood up and emptied his pockets into the tray. Once he had finished, she brought what looked like a gown, a head protection and slippers and asked Frank to wash thoroughly his hands and change into these. As soon as he had finished changing, she told Frank to ask for his belongings at the reception after the procedure. She came and took him to the operating room. Two doctors were already waiting, and they didn't say anything for some time, finally the male doctor asked questions to confirm Frank's identity and asked if he knew and been told about the procedure. He introduced himself and his colleague and asked Frank to sit on the operating bed. The male doctor took a clip board and ticked some boxes and left the room. The female doctor took over, she explained the procedure, it was to be a 30minutes max procedure, a small hole will be drilled on the hip bone and bone marrow extracted. He will be awake and there won't be pain. She paused for some time before continuing to explain the side effects. Localized pain and numbness at point of operation due to anesthetic but she emphasized this was to last a few hours up to a few days. She looked at Frank and asked if he had any questions.

"No, I don't have questions," said Frank.

"Ok the doctor will be back after a couple of minutes," said the female doctor and left the room.

"Can you lay down on your left side with your knees bent Mr. Frank," asked the male doctor as he entered the room.

For the first-time fear crossed his mind, he has never been in a situation like this before but as soon as he thought about Juliet he rests assured himself that this was for the best.

"I am going to give you the local anesthetic now, it might sting for a bit, but it will be okay after some time," said the doctor.

"Relax don't tense after a few minutes you won't be able to feel pain," added the doctor as he opened the cap protecting the needle and flicked the needle tip.

Some fluid escaped from the syringe into thin air and Frank felt a sharp pain that quickly disappeared. He felt the doctor rubbing his hip bone.

"Juliet, Juliet!" shouted Frank as he tried to run towards Juliet but for some reason he felt his legs very heavy.

He couldn't even move his legs, he tried running, and he fell but quickly got up. He never had experienced such a strange feeling before. He remembered feeling his head very heavy that he wanted to sit down. He could hear what sounded like an automated female voice from far away. Juliet stood there calling Frank to come by way of hand gestures. No matter how much he tried he didn't seem to get to Juliet, he had never felt like this before, he felt everything heavy. Soon he started finding himself further apart from the woman whom he thought was going to give him happiness. He sat on the operating bed, there was a lot of blood on the doctor's tray with bandages and the doctor's tools on the table. As soon as he saw the amount of blood in the doctor's tray he felt sick and lay down on the operating bed for some time. What time is it he asked himself, he lifted his left-hand to check he time, but he had no watch? Questions started running in his head, how long have I been here, what time is it, where are the doctors, why it seems dark in here? He felt dizzy and lied down for a bit. It has been 30minutes already it seemed very fast he thought to himself, but it sounded incorrect as outside was getting dark. Fear crippled him when he started thinking about Juliet he felt disoriented for some time. He wasn't clear what was going on he tried getting up again, he sat upright on the operating bed for a while. He felt his head heavy, what's going on he asked himself. He stood up looked in the doctor's tray, is this all my blood what happened did something go wrong all these are the questions that kept cropping to his head. He staggered and fell on one knee he felt all his energy drained.

"Juliet, I have to go," he told himself, he stood up and walked to the door, into the lift and down.

"Are you ok? Sir?" asked a lady in the lift.

Frank looked at her and acknowledged that he was ok.

"What time is it?" asked Frank supporting his head with his left-hand and sighed.

"Eh let's see," replied the lady in the lift putting her hand in her overalls pocket, she took out a small pocket clock and looked at it before she replied.

"5:45," Frank looked puzzled he didn't say anything he just looked at this lady in confusion.

"I mean quarter to Six," remarked the lady after noticing that Frank was confused, worried and surprised.

What happened, have I been to Juliet's already, I remember seeing her, did I talk to her, I don't remember that, but why am I still in these clothes, where are my clothes, where is my phone, where are my car keys, did I go to Juliet's and come back.

"Quarter to six, evening or morning?" asked Frank looking at the lady in the lift.

She smiled, looked at Frank and replied.

"Evening Sir," she paused for a while and continued.

"Are you sure you are ok Sir?" she realized Frank was

a bit confused, and she offered to help him.

"Can I use your phone?" asked Frank looking at the lady.

"Sorry Sir, I don't have it with me but ask at the reception they will be able to help you," as soon as she finished saying this to Frank, the lift doors opened, and Frank rushed to the reception desk on the ground floor.

"Please can I use your phone, it's important!" asked Frank in a raised voice. The receptionist lifted the handset and put it on the desk in front of Frank.

"We also have patient's free phones on level one above," she said whilst giving Frank some privacy. He lifted the handset and supported it with his left chin and shoulder.

He tried to put his hands in his pocket.

"Jesus!" remarked Frank.

He realized that he didn't know Juliet's number by head it was saved in his phone. He thought he can phone his friend but couldn't remember his phone number either. Jesus, what have they done to me he thought to himself he felt very afraid put the phone down and left the building as quickly as he can and headed for Juliet's house. He can't remember how he got to the area where Juliet lived he was a few feet away from Juliet's house. He had removed the hospital gown now only in his boxer shorts, he had felt his body so hot at one-point. He staggered to Juliet's house, he felt his legs very heavy but continued going. At last I am here, he thought to himself, he leaned against the door and pushed the bell. The thought of seeing Juliet made him forget his bad day, he smiled for a moment and waited for the door to open.

CHAPTER FOURTEEN

"What happened, where is he," asked the senior doctor entering the operating room.

"He is in a bad state, he lost a lot of blood, at one-point I thought we were going to lose him," said the junior doctor.

"Was the operation a success, you know what I mean," asked the senior doctor giving hand gestures as well.

"I had to do it on the lumbar, I had to remove part of his..., to fit it in, I don't know I am just afraid that he lost a lot of blood," the junior doctor replied whilst pacing up and down the operating room.

"So how long before we can initiate?" asked the senior doctor.

"Not sure, we had to sedate him heavily as well otherwise the pain could have put him in shock and above all you don't want him pointing his finger at you through the mirror at the police station. Would you want that?" the junior doctor paused and looked at the senior doctor who replied.

"No, we don't want that," the junior doctor continued.

"I thought so," he looked in the tray.

"Look at all that blood, it took me up to three hours, I haven't done this before you know?" remarked the junior doctor.

"We better find him, before we start...," said the senior doctor walking out of the operating room.

The junior doctor followed and asked a question.

"Is it not easier just to switch it on than to spend time trying to find him?" the senior doctor stopped and turned around facing the junior doctor.

"Do you have any idea how dangerous that could be right now, we must wait until the drugs are out of his system. Right now, he is confused, disoriented and doesn't have the energy to do anything let alone cope with this thing," the junior doctor kept quiet for a moment before talking to the senior doctor.

"But is it not the purpose of all this to boost his metabolism and see if this really work?"

He stopped and looked at his senior doctor who put his arm on his shoulder and said.

"Yes, but not after heavily sedating him, do you want to give him a heart attack?"

Juliet had a busy Friday as usual, she was looking forward to seeing Frank, she had plucked the courage and asked Frank on a date. She didn't want to wait she remembered her friend telling her to take her chances. She had everything she wanted apart from a decent guy. Since the day they met she had felt strongly about Frank. She couldn't wait anymore, she had waited all these university years now was her time to enjoy the best life must offer. That Friday she finished work at lunch time, she wanted to get her hair done and had some shopping to do. The time Frank phoned her asking if they can meet early she had already finished work, she had thought the same as well but because she wanted to make it special she had insisted they meet after 4pm that Friday. After work around 1pm she headed to a hair salon and had her hair done after that she drove to town to do some shopping. She bought some nice lingerie and a nice small dress that made her feel like a teenager, she remembered that she hasn't felt like this for a very long time. Meeting Frank had given her a boost and hope that at chocolates, new bed spreads, new pillows extra pajamas, extra bathing towels, shaving kit for men a shirt and shorts and a men's drove home to get ready to meeting Frank. future with Frank. She finished taking a bath and wore just the gown. She really wanted Frank to move in with her at any point, in the lounge, she thought to herself, no point of cooking her plans last, she had found her Mr. Right. After that she headed to the big lingerie she had bought and some high heels shoes and went to sit shaving her legs. She lay in the tub for a while thinking about her She arrived home and off loaded the car, she poured a glass of she had hoped that he would stay the weekend just the two of supermarket, she bought food for the whole weekend, wines, beers, the glass of wine close by took her shaving razors and started them. With the help of the shop assistant she loaded the car and were to eat out in some nice Italian restaurant to make the night wine and chose Celine Dion playlist. She entered the bath tub put special and one to remember. She felt sexy dressed in just lingerie, she looked herself in the corridor's big mirror, she touched both her breast, pushed them up, raised her eyebrows, smiled and turned ninety degrees and put both her arms on her buttocks, I need to tone down these a bit, so she thought to herself. She entered the lounge, she looked at her phone and discovered that she had a missed call, at one-point she thought it was Frank she quickly scrolled down her phone and smiled. It was her best friend probably snooping to check how she was doing the day she was meeting the guy of her dreams. She took her phone and pressed it against her ear, she lay on the lounge couch just in her lingerie and high heels and waited for her friend to answer the phone. Whilst waiting for her friend to answer, she lifted her shaved legs, they look great she told herself whilst sliding down her left-hand fingers on her shaved left thigh.

"Hey how's it going? Excited?" asked Rosalina.

"Hey, it's great, I can't wait, I think I am going to have a wonderful time, I feel good about this!?" said Juliet still laying on the lounge couch.

Rosalina knew her friend was happy from the tone of her voice, she felt happy for her. At last she had found the right man for her.

"So, are you going to do it tonight?" asked Rosalina.

"What do you think I am?" asked Juliet in a hastily manner, she giggled and continued.

"I don't know but honestly if it happens it happens, I am not a teenager anymore." She paused before continuing.

"We are both adults after all I waited so long for this," they joked and laughed and after some time she put the phone down and went to the bedroom to dress up.

She picked the dress from the bed leaving the other

stuff she had bought on the bed. She removed the dress from the packaging but before she wore, it saw the man's shirt she had bought for Frank. A naughty thought struck her, she picked up the XL shirt, unbuttons it and tried it on. She fastened only the bottom button and walked to the mirror in high heels and just panties. She felt sexy and just imagined doing that when she is making breakfast for him. She looked like one of the lingerie models she had seen in the magazines. She finished dressing up, poured a glass of wine and waited for Frank to come.

Four o'clock, she checked her time, made sure everything was perfect and excitedly waited for Frank. Four-seventeen and still no sign of Frank, probably caught up in a traffic jam, she thought to herself. Half past four and still no sign of Frank, she picked up her phone and rung Frank's mobile, and to her surprise his phone was switched off. What have happened, doesn't look good, maybe he is still stuck in a traffic jam? It was rush hour, and she knew everyone was busy going home after work and probably Frank was one of the unlucky drivers. She started feeling uneasy, she remembered that he also sounded excited when they decided to meet, so why then was he late she pondered. After ten minutes she picked up her phone and phoned Frank again.

"Where are you?" she murmured.

An automated female voice can be heard saying that the phone was switched off, and she advised to try again later. There was no option of leaving the message otherwise she could have left one. She waited, poured another glass of wine but left it untouched on the table. She tried ringing Frank again, but his phone was out of the range, she couldn't believe what was going on. She felt sad for a moment, she had waited and looked forward to this day. Even if he wasn't interested why not just say so she asked herself? She sat on the couch for another hour and still no sign of Frank no phone call either. She picked up the wine glass that was on the table, drunk half of it, went in the bedroom, wore clothes and picked up her hand bag and back into the lounge, picked up the car keys and walked to the front door. She can't remember how she got into the car, but she was on her way to Frank's flat. It was after 6pm, she was on the road and it was already getting dark. She drove for a while worrying about Frank she had hoped this day to be the beginning of her happiness but was turning to be one of her saddest days. She drove hoping at least to talk to Frank even if he was no longer interested she longed to see him again. She at one-point thought Frank was the old-fashioned guy who is the alpha male, one keen to make decisions and make the first move. Probably, she thought this was the mistake she had made making the first move. This had given her comfort at least it was something she could change. She had spent all those lonely nights at university studying that she did not see any issues with making the first move. She saw the driver in front flashing lights on and off and she looked on her dashboard and flicked a switch, by this time it was getting dark. After ten minutes more of driving, she saw the university directional sign, she indicated left and turned, she remembered the first-time she met Frank it was at the university, she had felt like a teenager meeting Frank somehow, she knew he was right for her. Passing the university, seeing students enjoying life in bars and restaurants surrounding the university, this brought memories of life at university and the choices you must make. She had chased and prioritized her studies to any serious relationship and now she had the chance to priorities her happiness with Frank. She stopped at the red traffic light and picked up her phone she dialed Frank's phone, but it was still switched off. She heard a horn made by the driver behind her, she looked in her rear-view mirror but couldn't see much as she was dazzled by the driver behind she tried to adjust her rear-view mirror before she heard another horn. She looked at the lights they were green, she put her car in first gear found biting point and put her handbrake down and moved the car slowly adjusting her rear-view mirror. She turned right indicated left and stopped outside Frank's flat. She got out of the car quickly leaving the car keys inside and went straight to Frank's flat door. The lights were off to her surprise if he is not home too then where is he, she asked herself. She rang the doorbell and waited for a while, there was no reply, and she walked straight to her car and opened the door without getting in, she reached for the passenger seat and took her phone. She rang Frank's phone again but still it was switched off. She reached for her purse on the passenger seat and took a pen and a note, she scribbled something down and went back to Frank's flat door. She put the note through the letter hole, knocked the door and rung the bell again but still no answer. She stood there for at least ten minutes without knowing what to do. She didn't know Frank's friends or anyone, all they had talked about was how they find very attracted to each other. Frank had told her where he lived that same afternoon when he tried to ask her to meet early, he had suggested spending the day at his flat, but she had declined insisting on meeting after 4pm as planned. She waited for another ten minutes before walking to her car.

"Darling, where are you?" she opened the car door and sat inside with her thoughts running world.

CHAPTER FIFTEEN

Meanwhile Frank's was still outside Juliet's house waiting, he had thought that she was going to wait for him but also so the possibility that she might have drove to his flat to find out why he had not turned up as planned. He knew she was determined to give this relationship a chance. This was the first-time he had not taken the lead, he believed somehow Juliet was not going to give up without answers. He had waited for at least an hour, he remembered the way she smiled, her smile was infectious she was beautiful and knew she was what he wanted. He felt very warm to his surprise, it was night time, and he had no clothes he should be worried about getting cold not feeling warm. He was tired, he remembered he had not eaten anything since the previous night, he felt his energies draining slowly, he got up and staggered walking away towards the street looking for help from the neighbor's at least they might help him in contacting her. He touched his forehead and wiped sweat with the back of his palm, staggered a few steps and entered the neighbor's house and rung the bell and waited. He felt his legs and head heavy and sat down for a while hoping someone opens the door. He rang the doorbell again but there was no answer, he staggered out of the neighbor's property and went in the direction where the loud music was coming from. He remembered feeling very weak and his legs very heavy, he remembered a woman lifting his head, he remembered someone shouts for an ambulance he remembered seeing people gathered around and a very sharp pain. People gathered around to see what was happening, there were reports that a half-naked man was found collapsed a few blocks from the house that was having a birthday party. There were reports that he might have taken some legal highs, and he was finding it very hard to breathe. The house where the party was being held had a large swimming pool and people had thought that probably he had felt hot and went for a swim before wandering outside. No one who had gathered couldn't identify him, the ambulance came, and he was rushed to hospital but pronounced dead on arrival. Juliet had waited for Frank in her car, she had tried several times to ring Frank but without success, she had phoned her friend Mary, telling her about her situation and Mary had suggested that she went back to her place and wait for Frank. She got in her car and drove towards university, she stepped on gas and rushed home. If it wasn't for her friend she was determined to wait at his flat for another hour, in her mind she had not thought Frank could have stood her up unless he had another girlfriend, she had wanted to surprise him and confront him, but her friend's explanation made more sense, maybe he had been caught up in traffic, probably had a blown-up tire and maybe his phone battery was dead, these are all the logic explanations that kept creeping in her mind. It felt like a few minutes and she was in her neighborhood, she remembered nearly being hit but an ambulance as she approached the major road leading to her house. She had stopped and had given the ambulance right of way at the last minute, at that point fear entered her mind but it was highly unlikely that Frank could have been in there, what for, he was full of life the morning they spoke on the phone. She continued driving and passed people gathered outside a house where loud music was coming from, she drove slowly but passed those people and went straight to her house. She was hoping to see Frank standing outside her house since talking to Mary, she had been hopeful, she had planned to just ignore the delay and continue as if nothing had happened. She saw a man standing outside her neighbor's house and thought that was Frank, she drove quickly indicated left and entered her driveway. She stopped the car quickly put on parking brake and came out of the car quickly and rushed towards that man. It was dark enough not to see that the man was her neighbor Mr. Octavo, as she approached him she noticed that it was Mr. Octavo. She stopped and cursed, she felt like crying, she said in a raised voice.

"Where is he?"

Mr. Octavo on hearing this walked towards her and greeted her.

"I just came back from work and saw a group of people gathered there," he pointed down the street towards the house that was holding a birthday party and looked at Juliet who appeared miles away.

She stood there, lost in her mind not even looking at Mr. Octavo.

"Sorry, what," she asked looking at Mr. Octavo.

"You know nowadays the world has gone crazy, young kids, taking drugs and ending up dead. It's a shame they waste their lives for nothing," he paused and shook his head before continuing.

"I just heard that one of the party goers collapsed and had to be taken by ambulance," he looked at Juliet and continued.

"He was found outside half-naked, boiling," he stopped and moved close to Juliet.

Juliet looked at him and said.

"I saw people standing outside on my way here but had no idea what happened."

Mr. Frank, looked towards where the man was found and said.

"There are rumors that he took legal highs, felt very hot took off his clothes jumped into the swimming pool probably to cool himself and wandered outside afterwards before collapsing," they stood there for a while talking and Juliet rung Frank's phone hoping that maybe he will pick up this time but still no answer.

She didn't think even for a minute that the man who was carried by the ambulance was Frank, it was not just logically possible. She rushed inside and for some strange reasons hoped to see him inside. She checked all rooms for Frank before pouring wine in a glass sipped some and sat on the couch. It felt like the worst day for her, she felt she had pushed Frank, who was still at the university and probably didn't want any relationship now. Probably that was his way of saying that he wasn't interested but at the same time felt it wrong to turn her down because he had phoned her that morning asking if they can meet earlier. She sat there sipping wine and trying to piece all things together. The logical explanation that put her mind to rest was that that Frank was seeing someone although he sounded excited he had prioritized the other lady. He liked her that was not in any doubt, no, but probably he wanted to juggle the two ladies at the same time, hence his morning's phone call asking to see her earlier in the afternoon and later spend the night with the other lady. She had made the first move and asked him out probably he had felt embarrassed and felt it inappropriate and rude to turn her away.

Anywhere this was not the first-time she had been stood up although this time it really hurts than the first-time. She had realized that Frank was younger than her and him being young probably didn't want a woman older than him. The more she thought about this the more she felt sad, she picked up her phone and rung Frank's phone again. If he was home and not with another girl probably by now, he should have charged his phone battery, so she thought. The phone was still switched off after another half an hour, she tried to ring Frank, but this time stopped herself. She felt Frank was deliberately avoiding her, she threw the phone against the lounge wall, it fell in pieces, battery there, the back lid on another side and the main phone on its own, screen shattered. She tried to hold down tears, but she felt a warm tear dripping down her left cheek and watery mucus coming down her nose and slowly onto the ridges of her lips onto her chin and onto the table. She sobbed, and she poured another glass of wine, and downed half down her throat before she cried herself to sleep on the couch.

"Where are you my love?" she asked.

CHAPTER SIXTEEN

JT was in his office and it was business as usual. He had been very busy lately as he was opening a new company. He had been traveling around the country for the past month looking for business ventures. He was determined to make his wealth grow even bigger by acquiring several businesses. He wanted to dominate every aspect of life, he had invested in the technology with several of his companies making latest gadgets, software, weapons and internet technology. He had invested in companies making artificial organs Companies in biological research. He had companies in insurance services providing life insurances, car insurances, home insurances and all kinds of insurances you can think of. He had shares in oil companies. He had donated several funds towards research at several universities and hospitals. Whenever he heard of an interesting development, he wanted to be involved and take control by investing funds. He had heard about Professor Anya's research the day he visited the university and had without hesitation invested funds into the research. He offered her and her team full-time jobs whilst she was still at the university. This is the kind of man JT was. He never ignored an opportunity that was his main key to success. In the past months he had been abroad investing in oil companies. Locally he had funded local hospitals and had written countless checks for local charities. JT had inherited his father's millions at the tender age of 22 and had bought shares in oils, software and technology to much success. He had acquired several businesses and over the years his fortune had grown hugely. He had a lot of influence, he kind of use his wealth to influence people around him he didn't hesitate to write checks if he sees the idea beneficial to him. He had married his childhood sweetheart at the age of 19 and they had been blessed with a beautiful baby girl. In the office JT was talking to his PR, Romeo.

"Sir the university had invited you to attend the opening ceremony of a new research lab named after you," he paused and looked at JT who pushed his hair backwards with his left-hand before lighting a cigar.

He walked to the glass door and opened a small window looked outside whilst puffing his cigar. His PR Romeo continued.

"They said the new lab is in your name to thank you for the grants you donated," he paused for a reaction from JT who puffed his cigar one more time, looked at him and replied.

"Oh yes see," he paused puffed more and continued.

"I am funding a lot of projects around the country, I was very fortunate and very luck and this is the little I can do towards a brighter future for our kids," he paused and looked outside through the oval glass door.

JT had a dream to rule the world one day. He had seen what technology can do. He had witnessed amazing achievements. He knew the time will come for him to realize his dreams or at least try. His latest research project, done by the underground bunker team had produced promising results in achieving something. They had successfully increased energy levels and metabolic functions in baboons. He talked to his PR Romeo for some time before his secretary interrupted them.

"Sir there is an important call for you can I put this through for you or ask them to phone you back later," asked his secretary.

"Who is it?" asked JT.

"Sir, he didn't say he said I should tell you that you were expecting this call and it's important," she said and waited for JT's reply.

"Ok put him through a secure line," remarked JT gesturing at his PR that he was dismissed, as he wanted to take this call in private.

The PR Romeo left the room and JT put off his cigar and walked to his chair sat down and picked up the receiver and spoke with an authoritative voice.

"Yes, what seems to be the problem," asked JT putting his legs on the table leaning back on the chair. The man on the phone said something that seemed to unsettle JT that he quickly removed his legs from the table and sat up straight in his chair. They spoke for a while and after the call JT stood up and walked up and down for a while, he lit his cigar again and walked towards the window and puffed up his cigar. At the university Brian had tried contacting his friend to ask how the date with Juliet had gone but couldn't get through and thought that he was at Juliet's enjoying life. He himself usually spend cozy nights with his girlfriend Melissa and he knew how at times you just want to be with someone you love alone just the two of you. He had been at Frank's flat the following day, but he wasn't home, and he had assumed he was still at Juliet's. Calvin had been to Frank's flat on Sunday the day they normally go to the gym, but he wasn't home he tried ringing his phone number, but the phone was still off. One week passed without anyone knowing the whereabouts of Frank. It was on Friday and normally Friday's Brian knew Frank had no lectures, so he went to his flat to see if he had been back. Still there was no sign of him and his phone was still off, it seemed odd and out of character but thought that he was still with Juliet. He had mentioned their meeting with Juliet and hinted on spending the weekend with her but not the whole week. He worried for some time and decided to go to the university to find out if he had been attending lectures for the past week. At the university some students doing same program as him informed him that they haven't seen him in lectures. He had assumed that probably he was staying with Juliet but still attending lectures. He had never met Juliet and didn't even know where she lived nor, had he had her contact details. He just waited for his friend to call. The second week passed by without any sign of Frank he tried ringing his phone, but it was switched off. He started worrying as he had put himself in Frank's shoes and found it hard that he would not make any form of contact after his fist date with Juliet, it was just not normal he must have called just to let him know how the date had gone. He went and checked at the university if Frank had attended the lectures but still there was no sign of him. He filed a missing student report at the university who later contacted the police. He went to ask the estate agents Frank was renting the flat from if Frank had recently contacted them, but Frank had not according to them. He explained that he was now worried about his friend and that he had filed a missing person report, they looked for the spare keys and went to the flat with Brian as he was trying to find clues of the whereabouts of his friend and Juliet's details. At Frank's flat he went through his stuff to try to find out Juliet' s details especially her surname so that he will try to find her. There were no clues, so he went to the university as he remembered Frank telling him that they met at the university, but he remembered also that Frank had informed him that she had finished her degree program the previous year, was she studying at this university or another university, how many Juliet's might have finished their degree program the previous year, what was she doing at this university and who or which department she had visited, was it personal or she was still involved in research? These are the questions that seem to have been worrying Brian. He didn't know Juliet's last name, and this meant going through all Juliet's who graduated the previous year, first search for Juliet from his university if not then from other universities. Two more weeks passed and there was no sign of Frank, Brian had contacted Frank's parents, and he had informed them about his disappearance with a lady called Juliet. He asked them if they have heard about Juliet and they recalled him telling them that he had met someone, but that's all he had said.

CHAPTER SEVENTEEN

Frank was taken to a different hospital than the one he had been before that afternoon; on arrival he was pronounced dead. His file was completed, and notes were written down suggesting it was an accidental drug overdose related death, he was found at a party half-naked without any ID's, His death was put down as not suspicious although later it was discovered that he had wounds on his back consistent with a hospital operation. They looked at all recent patients they had but there was no record of Frank and further tests were done to identify his body. After 5 weeks of disappearance presumably with Juliet the hospital identified Frank as the university student who was missing. Dental records had confirmed his identity and his close relatives were informed. They informed them that he had died from a drug overdose although post mortem results were inconclusive, there were no traces of any legal highs found in his systems or any kinds of drugs. His body had shut down when he was still alive, and he had experienced high temperatures before falling unconscious synonymous with a drug overdose. On hearing this his parents didn't believe that such an intelligent student would end up taking drugs especially knowing the dangers associated with these drugs. They were informed that he was found at a party and no one at that party knew him. His father rejected this explanation of his son's death. It was just not Frank, he was not a person who would go that route, he had everything planned, and he had a brighter life ahead of him. His father had requested his body so that he can have his son's body examined privately. His father was always suspicious about the government. His death was like a doubled edged sword piercing his father's heart. His death was unbearable he felt lost, and they wept for their only child. Brian was traumatized by his friend's death and like Brian's father didn't believe the explained cause of death although it was a possibility that Juliet might have influenced his decision as well. He was relieved at last that he had found a clue in locating Juliet. He contacted the hospital where he had been taken and asked about Juliet's whereabouts. He had thought that Juliet had been with Frank when he was taken by the ambulance to the hospital after he collapsed but to his surprise there was no record of Juliet or anyone with Frank the time he was found. The police had investigated and there were no leads about his friends or girlfriend among those who were at the party the night he died? No one of all the people who were at the party knew him? He was in his boxer shots and no clothes or ID's were found at the party belonging to Frank. Brian membered Frank telling him that Juliet had her own house, and that she had graduated the previous year, so he looked for graduates named Juliet who owned a house in the neighborhood. He went to the police and council offices looking for help and at last he managed to locate a one Kristian who lived in that area. Since the day Frank stood her up Juliet had kept herself busy with work trying to forget the incident although it really hurts. She had looked forward to spending time with Frank. She had not thrown away all the stuff she had bought for him. Although it sounded silly to her she had hoped that Frank would come to her or phone her to apologize or at least explain what happened that night. Days had passed by and there was no sign of Frank, no phone call or anything, his phone was still switched off. She had tried ringing him the following weekend just to see if he was ok but couldn't get hold of him. Her friend Karolina had visited her and spent that weekend comforting her. She hadn't moved on, but she knew there was not going to be a relationship between them. She kept herself busy trying to forget, and it helped although she had spent some night drinking wine alone still thinking about that night. One day she was in the bath and her phone rung, she just thought it was a call from work as she had been receiving these lately. One thought in her head made her think that possibly it was Frank as she had done for the past weeks only to find out that it was one person or another from the office. She continued taking her bath and after she had finished, she looked at her phone and found out that someone had rung her and left a message which informed her that if she knew Frank then to call the caller as soon as possible as it was important. She picked up the phone and phoned the person who had left the message, she felt relieved that at last she was going to find out why Frank stood her up and his whereabouts, and why he had switched off his phone. It never crossed her mind that something bad had happened to Frank. Brian had been investigating his friend's death, it was a real shock, and he was saddened and wanted to find out what had happened.

He had visited the area where his friend had collapsed to look for his car, no one had located his car anywhere. He couldn't find his car and the hospital had used his dental records to identify him. No ID's, credit and debit cards were found nor his phone which was still missing, and his car keys were not found either. He had spoken to the woman who found him outside the house which was hosting a birthday party. She had explained how distraught and disoriented he was and how he failed to breathe. She was sure he had taken drugs as he was boiling as she recalled. She remembered that he had mentioned the name Juliet but said nothing more. He started to put the pieces together, he realized that probably his friend was looking for Juliet's house. Was he lost did he not see Juliet? Did Juliet do this to him? If he was with Juliet why she did not go with him to the hospital? Where were his clothes and why was he half-naked? These are the questions that kept coming to his head. He probably thought that he was with Juliet, they spent time together that could explain why he was half-naked so probably he went outside for fresh air after making love to Juliet. Another thought came to him, it only makes sense if Juliet had picked him up from somewhere and he had packed his car left all his stuff inside and went to Juliet's house. That could explain why they couldn't find his car, so he realized Juliet had all the answers. A female voice on the other end was Juliet who confirmed that yes it was her, she knows Frank before she asked what was this about to which he refused to say over the phone and instead asked her if he can come to her house and talk to her of which she agreed to. He didn't say anything about Frank's death to Juliet because he thought she knew already since she was with him but couldn't understand why she didn't go with him in the ambulance day he collapsed. Only meeting Juliet and talking about this will provide answers to what happened to Frank that Friday afternoon. Juliet didn't sound surprised he thought Frank had sent his friend to explain why he stood her up at least she was happy and excited, probably Frank had sent his friend to explain and apologies for not turning up. She wondered what this was all about and waited for Brian to arrive.

CHAPTER EIGHTEEN

The news of his death spread the campus like veld fires and it came as a shock to all of them especially after being told that he had died of a drug overdose. Those who knew him knew that this was out of his character that instilled doubt in the minds of many. Frank had openly denounced legal highs in the past, and the university student union leaders had visited the hospital to ask for his autopsy. They had got his father's signed permission, and they had been refused to see him as the hospital implied that since he had been dead for weeks now his body was in a bad state. They finally got the autopsy and there was no trace of any illegal or legal drugs in his system. So how come that they suggest that he died from legal or illegal highs taken at a party. No one at the party knew him and no ID's or his documents were found, and his car was still missing. Although the autopsy hinted that the way he died was like those who have died of a drug overdose. His body had shutdown to prevent further damage to his organs, and the doctors had suggested that he might have taken a legal high which they didn't know about or that his body somehow eliminated the traces of the drug from his system. They were not sure if it was an illegal or legal high but one fact that was for sure was that it was not detected by the current methods. They hinted that it was common knowledge that some drugs are not detected or are quickly expelled from the body just before the person died. The hospital had refused to release his body for private test or burial as they had indicated that they wanted to do further test which was met by stiff opposition by the student leaders who saw it as a way of trying to cover up keeping the body to a state that it will be impossible to do any test. The student leaders had noted that there was a rise in deaths of educated highly influential students and non-students alike. People who were gifted and people who stood for something, people not afraid to challenge the norms and bad practices. They thought that the government was trying to eliminate the future leaders, the gifted leaders of tomorrow the young and inspiring people, students and non-students alike. By the time they agreed to release the body it was in such a bad state that he was buried within hours and there was no viewing. The students started riots demanding answers why students and other people were dying unexplained deaths and some missing. They were soon joined by the public that they started marching to town demanding answers. Juliet opened the door after hearing the knock on the door and saw Brian standing outside who introduced himself and reminded her that they had spoken on the phone. She invited him into the house and offered any refreshments, and he said.

"I'm sorry about Frank," and asked for a glass of water and if he can use the bathroom first. She replied to Brian.

"It's okay, but I was really upset for the past weeks," she showed him the bathroom and went in the kitchen to get water for him.

She thought Brian was apologizing to her for being stood up by Frank. He entered the bathroom and used the toilet he walked to the sinks washed his hands and looked into the mirror. He took water from the tape using his hands and splashed it onto his face and gently wiped it downwards. He knew why his friend was crazy about Juliet, she was beautiful, with a well-built body, and he remembered telling himself that she seemed like a very good person. He saw in the mirror a man's shirt behind him too big to be hers. He thought to himself, he realized that Frank was at her house, it seemed like the shirt belonged to him, it was his size XL. He saw a man's gown, slippers and shaving kit. So, he thought to himself, Frank was here, so it made sense he tried to put the pieces together. Frank was here, so they made love and, in his shorts, went outside, probably collapsed and was taken by ambulance before she realized that he was missing that makes sense, so all his stuff must be here, and Juliet must know the whereabouts of his car. He kept thinking about this until he heard Juliet speaking to him.

"Sorry, but are you ok in there," she asked after realizing that Brian had been in there for some good minutes. She couldn't wait, she had a lot of questions that needed answers.

"I will be out in a minute," shouted Brian as he was

closing the water tap.

He came out of the bathroom and stood for a while inspecting the whole lounge room and peeping into the bedroom.

"Please sit down and here is the water you asked for," she sat down herself and pointed to the glass of water on the table.

He looked around for a minute then looked at Juliet and said.

"Sorry thank you," he lifted the glass of water and drunk all the water at one go and gave a burp to which he apologized and said.

"Where is Brian's car and his belongings?"

She looked puzzled and said.

"Car? I don't know why you ask," he looked at her and repeated the question to which she apologized and replied that she didn't know where his car was.

"Was Frank not driving his car that Friday you had a date with him?" she looked even more puzzled but now realized that something had happened. His line of question was a bit odd a strange feeling ran down her spine and she felt a little upset she thought Frank had sent his friend to apologize and make a stupid excuse.

"Is he okay, why you ask about his car. Is this some kind of joke? Is this an excuse asking me about his car? Is this the way he apologies for letting her down by not turning up?" he looked at Juliet who at this time seemed really upset he looked puzzled himself and said.

"I thought you said you were upset for the past weeks," he sat up straight and leaned forward facing Juliet who replied.

"Yes of course I was upset for the past weeks, your

friend stood me up?" there was a moment of silence, Brian looked even more worried.

"Did you not know?" he asked Juliet who replied in a soft low voice.

"Know about what?" she asked Brian.

He realized that probably Juliet didn't know he was dead. He looked confused he started thinking to himself, so he was here, and he left, and she thought he stood her up, but still it does not make sense she can't say he stood her up when he was here at one-point unless... he didn't finish thinking before he looked at Juliet, stood up and sat next to her and said.

"Were you with Frank that Friday," he paused looked at Juliet and continued.

"That Friday he died," he didn't even finish his sentence before Juliet screamed and started crying uncontrollable.

He hugged her, and they cried together. Juliet remembered that ambulance that nearly bumped into her on her way back, she blamed herself for leaving that day. Frank had been to her house if she hadn't left probably she might have helped him she might have saved his life. If she had stopped when she saw those people outside the house where he was found probably she might have helped. She cried even worse when she realized that Frank liked her very much, she had given up because she thought Frank loved someone else. How unfair that her love be taken away from her in such circumstances. Just like Brian she had so many questions that needed answers. Where were his clothes where was his car and wallet and keys? She blamed herself, Frank really loved her, she did her best she did what she thought was right at the time but still blamed herself for not trusting Frank. If she had trusted Frank that day she could have drove home as soon as she had found out that he was not at his flat. If she hadn't thought that he had another girlfriend she might have drove home straight away and she might have found Frank outside her house waiting for her. She might have taken him to the hospital instead of someone else having to find him collapsed outside. His death brought so many questions especially the manner in which this happened, together with Brian they teamed up in trying to find the missing pieces.

CHAPTER NINETEEN

JT is on the phone and he seems unsettled by something, he is pacing up and down in his office, he stopped for a while and walked to the oval glass door and looked at the view outside.

"Ok we can't talk this over the phone, meet me tomorrow 7pm same place. ok?" he said in a high voice and put the phone done.

He called his secretary after making the phone call and told her to cancel all appointments after 6pm and asked her to get the limo ready. Things were not going well as JT had anticipated, he had hoped that by this time everything would be going well as he had planned. He had waited a long time for this and he had invested a lot of money. He wanted to dominate the world in every sense of the word. He wanted to establish a new order, an era in which he was the dominant force. He wanted to impose new rules,

rules everyone will obey or perish. He had a vision when he is the ruler, telling people what to do and them obeying. He had communist view, he had studied Stalin in a great deal during his college years. He had been fascinated by Stalin's views, he had believed that to achieve anything in society there must be a central command and everyone else obeying that command. He knew in nowadays society that was impossible with human rights campaigners and freedom of speech activist that was never going to be a success. He had worked so hard over the years, he had injected a lot of money into different projects and at last he was about to realize his dreams. At 6pm JT's limousine left his office and headed for the City, with his secretary inside beside him. Clara was a blonde lady, of medium built, she had a beauty mole on her left side where her nose ends. She had blue-gray eyes and a sexy smile, she was a little shy at first until you get to know her. She had boobs of a goddess not too big and not too small just perfect. She wore reading glasses and normally tied her hair in a ponytail. She had worked for JT for a very long time, she was loyal to JT, and understood the man JT was and what he needed. She had a small sexy voice, she had always been there when JT needed a special favor. She had on a drunken night had spent some quality time with JT the first days she started working for JT, but it was a one off and ever since she had been going out with a singer and producer from New York, Brooklyn called TK and they have a baby girl together. Lately there have been rumors that TK had been dating Clara's friend Miley. JT is in the limousine with his secretary Clara, he lit his cigar and asked the driver to open the roof door of the limousine.

"Do you mind?" he asked his secretary Clara as he showed her the cigar.

"No, it's okay Sir, you can smoke," she looked at JT whilst pulling her miniskirt down.

JT lit his cigar and puffed it and blew the smoke upwards towards the open sunroof of the limousine. He looked at Clara and touched her thighs.

"So, you still with your man, what's his name again?" remarked JT looking at Clara.

"It's complicated Sir, he is TK, I think he's seeing someone else," said Clara, she paused for a while took off her reading glasses, wiped her eyes with the back of her right hand.

"I can't trust man anymore Sir, I have been hurt, just imagine I gave him a beautiful daughter, and he is never there?" she paused and looked at JT before she continued.

"Last year we spent Christmas alone, and this year Easter went by without any sign of him," she looked upset and looked at JT.

There was a moment of silence the engine of the limo was the only noise that was heard as they headed to the City. JT puffed his cigar once more and removed his hand from Clara's legs and hold her left shoulder.

"I think he loves you, maybe he is just busy, these musicians they never settle at one place," he tried to comfort her, he remembered all these years she had worked for him.

She was like family now, in fact they spent most of the time together, he remembered all those years he spent more time with Clara than with his wife. She was always there even out of work hours as he holds numerous meetings in hotels and night clubs. She was also there; she had sacrificed her personal time to attend meetings with JT. He reminded Clara that on several occasions TK had interrupted their meetings demanding to take her home to their beautiful daughter. At one-point TK had punched JT when she confessed they had a drunken one-night stand with JT a few weeks after she started working for him years before she met TK.

"Remember that day my bodyguard nearly shot your boyfriend?" he looked at Clara and smiled.

"I swear that was stupid of him but also that also proved that the guy loved you," there was one incident when TK came back home to find out that Clara was not home, and he went to the Hotel in the City where JT was having a business meeting.

He entered the Hotel and went straight in the conference room once inside he went to Clara and grabbed her by her wrists and dragged her out. JT stood up and tried to explain and before he knew it, TK had already punched him in the face. JT's bodyguard pulled his gun in seconds of the incident and pointed it at TK who moved forward and shouted.

"Shot if you want, this is the mother of my daughter, she has a young daughter, do you understand that," it was JT who raised his hand to his bodyguard to stop otherwise TK could have been shot.

No one had ever touched JT and walked away, JT felt like Clara was family, after the incident he had not asked Clara to do too many unsocial hours. JT had a reputation of being ruthless, many people had disappeared, and he had been known to shoot people not loyal to him himself.

"I am tired Sir, too many lonely nights, he is never home, I have been told he is going out with another lady," she looked upset trying to get JT's sympathy.

He looked at her and put his arms around her and said.

"You have to understand man are always like that, me for example, my wife complains too. Look I spend most of my time doing business deals I leave home early and I go back very late," he puffed his cigar and continued.

"Last week I came back home and found her crying, she said she was lonely and I should buy her a dog," he paused, puffed his cigar and continued talking to Clara.

"You just reminded me, tomorrow find out where I can get a puppy for her," the car drove towards the City as they spoke.

"I promised to take her to our special restaurant this weekend," he looked at Clara and puffed his cigar, she looked at him and opened her purse she wrote something down and the limo cruised towards the City.

The limo arrived at the night club just before 7pm, they got out of the limo and she took her handbag some files and JT's suit jacket.

"Anything else you need Sir?" she asked JT whilst stood behind the limo back door. She had picked up JT's jacket from the limos back seat.

JT always wore suits even after hours, he normally wore cross bands with suits and a tie. He had nearly two wardrobes full of suits. He had a personal tailor who brought new suits every month to fill the whole wardrobe. He had numerous shoes but because he liked dark colors, it seemed as if he never changed shoes, but in fact he changed shoes like socks and he liked expensive Italian pointed shoes. They entered the hotel where the receptionist welcomed them and informed him that they were all there and all had arrived 15minutes early. JT demanded punctuality he was known to cancel meetings when the other party arrived even just on time. He liked to come and find everyone waiting for him before the meeting. He entered the meeting with Clara and everyone stood up, he walked to his central seat and sat down and asked everyone to sit down. They all sat down, and it was business as usual. It lasted about 45 minutes and they all left. JT asked Clara to order some food and champagne, they all left the conference room to the hotel restaurant. They ate food and drunk wine as they talked after they have finished eating they went outside and as usual Clara got the champagne and entered the hotel taxi which was waiting whilst JT got into the limo. She waved goodbye to her boss, and the taxi left, JT's limo drove for about 20mins and stopped to pick up someone. A man in his forties entered the limo, he was wearing glasses and dark clothes.

"We tried Sir, but it wasn't a success, we are not sure what was the problem," he paused and looked worried and looked at JT.

"Operation was successful, but he lost a lot of blood and when we tried to test if it works his system rejected it, his body shutdown, and he was overheating. He fell unconscious and died on arrival, we have all concluded that it was too early to initiate soon after the operation," JT nodded his head and looked at the man he was talking to before asking him.

"What do you think is the waiting time from date of operation?" he looked at JT and there was a moment of silence before he replied.

"So far we have agreed a month minimum waiting time. This gives the body time to adjust," JT looked disappointed but optimistic that he has to wait for weeks to see if this works.

CHAPTER TWENTY

Professor Anya after she lost her job she went to her parent's house in the countryside to relax and think about her future. As she sat home one day watching television she heard on the news about Frank's death, and she had noted deaths in the past similar to this one. She recalls how her animal subjects had succumbed due to excessive body heat. She wondered if these were related but she found it was impossible since JT had closed the lab and dismissed everyone and after all, test on humans were 5 or more years far in the future because the tests had to be deemed safe on humans first and then passed into legislation and with all the bureaucracy involved the minimum the bill could be passed was 5 years. How come these people are dying like the monkeys in the lab. She read reports that earlier on in another city a man was seen running at extra ordinary speeds before he died of exhaustion. This is what they have been trying to achieve over the past 4 or more years. Another shocking report was of a baby born three months after she falls pregnant. This is exactly what they tried to achieve but their research had been unsuccessful. Are all these reports true? Is someone making up all these stories? If so for what reason? There were reports that a young boy claiming to be only a 2-year-old who was the size of a teenager was at the university research labs. He was very fast in his movements, he ran very fast and he was much smarter that other children his age, he analyzed everything like a computer. They concluded that he had suffered amnesia he didn't remember his age, but he was adamant that he was a two-year-old boy. His parents confirmed the same but were all regarded as having suffered amnesia and were held at the hospital. She believed them, this was the main goal of their research, but this was five or ten years in the future. There were the only ones who had tried this as far as she knew. If it's true, then who had achieved what they failed to do and how? This really intrigued her she wanted to see it for herself, she wanted to find out how this had happened. The next day she packed her bags and headed for the city. What an achievement she thought to herself but who and how, what did we miss over the years she kept thinking to herself? She was in the express high-speed train heading for the City, she took that day's papers to see if the story of a boy and his parents was in it. She turned to page seven and there it was. The reporter had indicated that an extraordinary boy was discovered with extra ordinary functions and was at the university where tests were being held. The doctors believed he had suffered amnesia and couldn't remember his date of birth but knew everything else. She scrolled down and found out that his parents were being held at the university hospital according to their will so further tests can be done. The parents also defended their son, it was no amnesia they had insisted that and the chance of the whole family having amnesia at the same time was never heard of. That alone raised questions and professor Anya knew what this was but never thought to witness such a miracle until maybe after five years. She looked at the name of the university hospital where the family was being held and checked for a contact name and contact telephone number. She took her phone out and dialed the number and waited for the answer.

"Can I speak to the person in charge of the family I read in the paper?" she asked and paused before someone on the other hand asked a series of questions.

"Are you a relative?" in which she replied no.

"Have you experienced the same or do you know someone who have?" she replied no again.

"I am afraid we cannot be of any help?" the person put the phone down straight away, the professor tried to talk something before she had the line gone dead. She dialed the same number and waited.

"Hello, how can we help?" asked the person on the other end.

"I am a professor I did similar research, but I can't talk over the phone, but I might be able to help," the professor tried her best to convince the person taking her call, the person on the other end, agreed and asked her phone number so that the person in charge can ring her.

"Can I come there later in the afternoon I think it's

something we have to talk about in person with the person in charge," she paused and waited for the reply.

"Ok I will tell you the address just hold on," she told the professor the address.

She arrived at the university hospital and spoke for more than an hour with the consultant concerned before she agreed her to meet the family concerned. In the interview room there were other 5 professionals from different backgrounds and as she entered the building with the consultant they all introduced themselves. The leading consultant briefly explained what was going to happen, the family was going to be brought into the room and each professional will have time to ask at least five questions. The questions had to be direct, and they had to highlight and try to resolve the age issue among others. They spoke to each other for some time before the family were introduced into the room. The family entered the room accompanied by the assistant and were asked to sit down. The boy asked if he can remain standing he said that he had been seated the whole day and was feeling tired and sleepy. The boy looked at everyone in the room and asked their names one by one. The leading consultant asked the first questions about the boys age and brief life history. When he heard this, the boy seemed upset and replied,

"No matter how many times you ask me my age I will still tell you the same as I told you before that I am 2 years, 8 months and 12 days old. I was born on 09 June at 18:07," he looked at everyone one after the other to make sure they all understood.

They all asked questions one after the other and they

were all surprised by the level of understanding and the responses he gave. They were really astonished they tried to find out if he had received training or education, but he hadn't. The parents explained that their son had a gift he was very fast and did extra ordinary stuff that the other kids were now refusing to play with him. They also highlighted that few days after his birth they at one-point thought that he had died. They explained that one day the mother woke up in the middle of the night after she had her son make some growling sounds to find her son in a pool of sweat and failing to breathe. She thought he had a fever, but she realized that his body seemed to be shutting down she quickly put ice from the freezer on his feet, he seemed to have died at one-point as he stopped breathing. After hours his body temperature came down to normal levels, but he did not wake up for days. He was breathing normal as long as the ice was left on his feet. After that when he woke up, he had grown up very rapidly he woke up and stated walking and talking to everyone's astonishment. His parents realized that if they tell anyone they might lose their son and above all no one would believe them. This had occurred again after 3 months, his body had overheated, and all his organs seemed to shut down he falls unconscious, and he slept for days as long as the ice was on his feet and when he woke up, he had grown up and even faster and smarter. After nine months he started leaving the house at night complaining that he was feeling hot and needed night the cool breeze and would not come back until the morning and he would sleep for days and when he wakes up, he would have grown up than what he was. The mother explained that one day she asked him what he does at night when he is outside, he told her that he run from one city to another or for long distances at extra ordinary speeds. After that he will feel very tired that he just wanted to sleep for days and when he wakes up, he will have grown much bigger. He never forgets things, and he solves problems and understand human emotions he just need to look at you to know what you going to say or what you want. Everyone looked astonished they all started talking to each other, the professor realized that when the boy's body overheat, that's when his metabolism will be changing and that cooling down was essential. She recalled years ago in the lab, trying to cover the whole body with ice as well when the monkey experienced high temperatures, but the monkey died within minutes. She noted that possible during her tests in the lab the monkey died because its body experienced sudden extreme temperature changes from very hot to very cold that has instantly stopped the metamorphosis and caused the sudden death. She remembers one day at the circus all those circus actors walking on fire without feeling pain and those actors walking on broken glass without showing pain. Ok she said to herself, the feet feel pain, but it gradually sends signals to the brain so ice on feet only is sufficient to control body temperature slowly over time. This was the breakthrough, so sleeping afterwards is the key that's when the changes occur no wonder why they didn't notice the changes. It seems all the major changes occurred after the sleep which is the key, so the answer is trying to make sure the subject survives the high temperatures and have enough sleep-in order to see the changes. She remembers expecting sudden changes soon after the test, but they were wrong the answer was not far away she noted. This reignited her at last she thought she will be able to convince JT to give her another shot. She thought to herself but who has managed to do this. She asked the consultant to meet the parents in private if possible in which she agreed. She took them outside to the playing grounds and started talking with them. She asked them which hospital the boy was born and if they remembered the name of the doctor who was in charge and to her surprise the boy remembered the name of the doctors and nurses who helped deliver him. She wrote their names down and left the university hospital heading home. At home she went straight to her computer and logged-on, she looked at all the reports of all the experiments they had done. Yes, high temperatures had been a problem in all subjects, she noted that they added ice to the whole body to cool down the subjects but in all cases, death was within minutes. Sudden temperature contrast might have killed the subjects instantly. She looked through the other reports dating back many years,

"That can't be," she said to herself scrolling down one report.

She noted that on one occasion they had run out of ice and there was only enough to cover the feet and she was surprised by the results. The monkey had survived for hours with a little ice on the feet until they added more ice to the whole body that it suddenly died. She noted how close they had been to achieving astonishing results many years ago. That night she couldn't sleep thinking of what might have been. If she had looked at all previous tests, they carried out they could have made a breakthrough, she blamed herself for the missed opportunity.

"Damn!" she exclaimed before continuing.

"We were that close, had we paid attention on that day."

She couldn't sleep that night, she tried to arrange an appointment with JT but refrained from making the phone calls just a few seconds before someone picked up the phone. This is far more important she thought to herself, this is what JT had wanted, this was JT's dream, and she thought any mention of a breakthrough will make JT cancel all important meetings and give her all his attention. One thought after another ran through her mind. This was her dream, she could be rich now, surely JT had been more than generous to her, over the years she was paid ten times more than her graduates friends. JT had secured a house, a car and everything she wanted whilst she was at university. She had a job whilst she was still at the university, and JT had treated her like a daughter, ever since because of that she had felt some connection to him. She believed JT had closed the project as he had invested a lot of money and probably he started feeling like he was wasting more money. This according to her was the main reason for pulling out the plug. She couldn't remember what time she went to bed as even in her sleep she was still thinking about this and what the future holds for her. This was the biggest breakthrough in human history and her studies had not only unlocked this but contributed a lot that could make her very rich, she was the head of the research team. She had worked with JT for years and had always obeyed him until a few months before closure. This was due to her objections to human testing without successfully tests on animals, she had refused to even think about considering this idea. JT had expressed disappointment but had come to the same conclusion as her that more tests had to be done before any human test. She had thought JT had agreed to this. This time she was going to prove and confess to JT fingers crossed that she was to agree to human testing. This little boy had convinced her that somehow it was safe to start human test. Even if this was JT's reason for closure, now he had every reason to reinvest in the project. What this means in terms of money and her future was beyond belief, she knew JT wanted this badly and would part with any money as long as he had his results. She couldn't stop smiling, at last she was to become so rich that she never needed to work again, JT was rich beyond belief, he nearly controlled the continent's riches, he had businesses everywhere.

CHAPTER TWENTY ONE

The death of Frank and the riots in the City with the resulting causalities had meant going back to the drawing table for JT and all his subordinates. A lot of people were shot dead by the City protectors that new laws were passed on to prevent death whenever there is a demonstration. The government ended up out sourcing protection and security services to a private company and JT took the opportunity to be responsible for law and order and protecting government and private property from demonstrators. One of his company was responsible for everything from security and protection of government property to protection of banks. Slowly he took over all services from the government. This has meant that he was in charge of security and protection and used his influence for the government to pass laws giving him more power and immunity. This meant in turn cleaning up his dirty secrets, he saw this as an opportunity to infiltrate all government organizations even more widespread. Over the years he had controlled most services and owned most companies and service industries. He was now employing most people in the whole continent. He had seen this as the breakthrough to his plans, everything was falling in the place like a jigsaw puzzle. This was his way of controlling humanity this was his dream. All he had to do was to find a way of making his plans through. After the riots in the City and the widespread deaths of a lot of protesters at the hands of the City protectors owned by the government people had voted that security be passed onto private companies as the people had lost trust in the government as they took things in their own hands. This was an opportunity JT was looking for, he had devised plans and had had sleepless nights now his dream was handed to him on a plate. He was too fast to notice opportunities and took all opportunities with both hands. It meant nearly using half his fortune, but this he saw it as an opportunity to make him the ruler of many. He employed most people in some countries if not all in all his employees were all asked to sign forms and go for medical screening. He had emphasized that he wished never to witness the riots of previous years and the loss of so much lives that he vowed to protect all his employees at any cost. This had won him the favor and trust as opposed to the government. The government had slaughtered their own people that day of the riots, the government was blamed for the deaths and disappearance of so many influential people. All this helped JT become one powerful man in the whole world. JT's research team had worked hard over the following years, they had stopped testing on adults which coincided with his taking of security and protection services from the government. This has meant him winning favor from the people that many people were working for him. The underground team had had a breakthrough. Even JT realized that it was safer to experiment on young infants and kids as their deaths in infancy would be believable and easily explained and can be easily covered up than that of a healthy grown up adult. JT had wanted results in months, but later acknowledged that his plan was likely to be achieved in few years to come and this made him authorize testing on new babies and creating babies this way. After the first-year since the death of Frank and the riots that followed there were numerous reports of miracle babies. There were never deaths of adults that were suspicious although there was a sharp rise of deaths among children the first-year, but this was quickly pointed out that it was due to a new bug that had been discovered. After the first-year the deaths stopped and there were miracle babies everywhere. The first was of a young boy whose parents suddenly died in a car crash three month after he was born. The day of the accident, the baby had stopped breathing, he had experienced high temperatures. It was three months after he was born, he was growing up fine, and it never occurred to the parents that there was something wrong with him until this day. It was a normal day like any other until that afternoon. The mother heard cries of the baby and rushed to the baby's attention only to find him having breathing problems she knew straight away that something was wrong, she called her husband, and they took the baby into the car and took him straight to the hospital. On the way to the hospital the baby suffered something like a seizure, his temperature had rose to extreme levels, the father panicked and increased the car's speed. As his wife was screaming holding their son in her hand, the father looked at them and that was the last time he saw them. They were involved in a head on crash that killed him instantly and left his wife for dead. It was minutes after the crashed that the wife died too and by the time the ambulance came the parents were all dead but surprisingly the baby suffered only minor bruising or, so they thought. He was rushed to the nearest hospital where he remained unconscious for days. His body temperature had remained high despite efforts to cool him down and was later pronounced dead after days in the intensive care. He had stopped breathing his body had shut down and all his vital organs had stopped functioning. It was not until they had put him in the mortuary that one worker had cries of a baby coming from the mortuary days after they had left him there. By the time he was discovered he had grown up, but no one had an idea about that because no one took much notice, the only people who could have noticed the change had all died. It was not until months' later that they started to understand what had happened. In the foster home where he was left, one day he stopped breathing and was rushed to the hospital where he had been before. He had died again, the doctors there did a lot of tests but to no avail, it was not until they had looked at his medical file when the picture imaged. The doctor who was responsible for him the first-time when he was brought to the hospital had noticed similarities to the first-time he had examined him. He suggested placing him in a temperature-controlled room, but nothing changed. They left him there for days and constantly checked upon him hoping that he might wake up and come to life. There were no changes until they put him in the mortuary again when he later woke up days later. He had grown much faster he was bigger than the first-time he had died. This astonished everyone, although it was not uncommon for people to wake up after they have been pronounced dead, this was a special case. Not only that he woke up but when he woke up, he was much alive full of life and had grown in size. He remembered everything, truly this was a miracle as this had never been witnessed before.

CHAPTER TWENTY TWO

The following morning the professor headed to the city after meeting the family who had a boy who was considered a miracle. She had a lot of questions that needed answers and was, excited about meeting JT. She didn't even phone JT's secretary to book an appointment as she had done all these years. JT was a busy man and would only agree to meet anyone by appointment no matter how important that person was. He was a strict man, he never seemed to break his rules. She remembered stories that he had refused to cancel business appointment to take his wife to the hospital instead sending his secretary to stand for him. He was very strict, and this was one of the reason he had acquired and maintained all his wealth. He barely spent time with his wife either, but the professor believed that this was a big, no matter what, JT would sacrifice his appoints just to hear her story. This is what JT had worked for all his life. This was his dream, surely after spending a lot of money on this project, he was bound to agree meeting the professor at short notice, so she thought. It was not long before she arrived at JT's office, she was nervous and excited as well she had a sleepless night just thinking about this. She couldn't wait to see the look on JT's face as she delivered the news to him about the breakthrough. She remembered those days she worked for JT she had missed those days. JT had made her feel really special she had seen herself working for JT forever only to be gutted when he pulled the plug. This was the best opportunity to keep her dream alive, she had to do her best to convince JT to restart the project. JT was a man in his own class, he had over the years developed his methods and put rules in place to achieving his goals and had never looked back. He was one of the strictest people she had ever met yet very generous to those he valued. At one-point one of those nights when he took her out to discuss business meetings she had imagined what life would be like to be married to such a powerful man, so powerful that he controlled everyone including all those in the government. Even if he was not in the presidential office he had accumulated wealth and power that he effectively made the decisions. It was every woman's dream to marry such a powerful man, but she knew JT considered her as a daughter. His own daughter had not been so ambitious as he had hoped that she would. She saw no reason of doing anything as her father was so rich that he controlled the whole world. She entered JT's office building, a lot had changed since the last time she had visited. Before you could walk straight into the building all you needed was to just sign with the security at the reception and speak to his secretary for appointment. This time everything was automated. You could not enter without iris scan, without finger print scan, without a reference number, without placing your hand on one of the machines there and without going through a body scan. There was no one at the door only automated machines. She was denied entrance, she had seen people come in and go. The whole world had gone mad she thought to herself, everyone was like a robot. They were having their eyes scanned, finger prints taken and were being searched before they were allowed to enter. She felt frustrated and asked for help to which all was refused and was told that she had to have clearance first before she was allowed inside. A lot has changed since she left. That massacre day of the riots had frightened everyone that security was taken seriously. It was not until later in the day that she met one of JT's worker who offered to inform JT that she wanted to see him. JT was in the middle of the meeting when her secretary approached him and whispered something in his ear. He paused for a while, for a minute he looked confused, a lot of questions were running through his mind, the professor, what is it now, what does she want, what has happened this time. JT had cleaned his acts or at least they thought so, he was responsible for the security of billions of people and a scandal was the last thing he wanted. His plan was only going to be successful as long as the majority if not all humanity had faith and trust in him. He had a lot to lose for the first-time in his entire life he felt threatened. He had remembered years back when he fell out with the professor over testing on human beings without following the necessary protocol. She had surprised him on that day; over the years he had treated her like his own daughter paying her ten times that what he was paying others. To him this was buying her cooperation, but she misunderstood that. That day he saw her as a threat, a threat to his plans, any leaked word that it was him responsible for all those deaths and not the government would send him crushing. He felt angry, he stood up paced up and down his office, he took his electrical cigar smoked for some time before going to his drawer and taking a small box from his drawer. He put the electrical cigarette down, paused a bit thinking before reaching inside the small box and pulling out a big normal cigar. Everyone in the meeting realized that something was wrong JT had never reacted like that to any time, this was big. They all offered to leave his office and promised to rearrange the meeting. For some time, he seemed as if he wasn't listening to them he was far away in his thoughts.

"Oh, okay reschedule the appointment with my secretary," explained JT as he walked to the glass oval window.

He lit his cigar and puffed it looking outside the window. After a few puffs he looked at the cigar and looked outside the window again. It was a long time since he had smoked a cigar. Since taking over security and protection of the whole continent he had emphasized on healthy life style. He was not to let some disease ruin his plan. He wanted to be in power as many years as he can this breakthrough had meant a better life much improved life for humanity. The voice on his answering machine informed him that the professor wanted to see him, and she was in the foyer. No one had turned up without any appointment and no one had disrupted JT's meetings. This had surprised JT the professor knew the rules, so why she didn't make an appointment, was she taking advantage? of him trying to blackmail him? What does she want? These are the questions that were going through JT's mind before he heard a knock on the door. The professor had expected the possibility that JT might refuse to see her on short notice as he had done all those years but as she sat in the foyer she saw everyone coming out of JT's office to her astonishment. This must be big she thought to herself maybe JT had been expecting me all these years, possibly he finally realized the mistake he had done when he pulled the plug off. She felt important as all those business men passed by leaving JT's office. This gave her more confidence as she realized that JT needed his more than anything else. She realized this was her only chance of bargaining with JT to get a piece of the cake. By the time JT's secretary Clara announced that JT could see her she had done a trip around the world in her own private jet. She stood up and quickly knocked the door. She did not wait for JT to tell her to come in but opened the door quickly and entered inside.

CHAPTER TWENTY THREE

It had been two years after the death of Frank. Brian had graduated from the university and had been lucky to have found a very good job soon after finishing his degree. The death of his friend had been a bitter pill to swallow. He had promised himself to find answers of how his friend had died. He still had a lot of unanswered questions, they had not found any of his belongings, even his car was never accounted for. He suspected foul play, but he had no leads. After his death he had been to the hospital where they took Frank that day they found him unconscious. He had been to the police, and they had searched for his belongings with no lucky. He had done his best to no avail. Frank never mentioned any appointment that Friday. Brian knew only that Frank was meeting Juliet that afternoon. The fact that Frank had rung Kristian wishing to meet earlier during the day that Friday and not at 4pm as they had planned ruled out the possibility of him having another appointment that

Friday afternoon or, so he thought. His best friend had not told him about the other appointment. So many questions remained unanswered, together with Juliet they had tried to piece things together but with no lucky. Frank never told Juliet or his parents about the other appointment at the hospital. Brian had been to all local and nearby hospitals asking for any information relating to Frank but had not found any clues. After the riots there had been a lot of changes in terms of security. It just made things hard for him. It was hard to get any information after that, he remembered going back to the hospital where his friend had been taken to the day he was found unconscious, and how hard the security made things for him. He had been blocked by the new security forces now present at the hospital. He remembered being held there for hours being interrogated before he was allowed to enter. His name and details were taken and recorded by the new security forces and had been given clearance after they made a telephone call to one of their bosses. All this didn't put him off, he wanted to find the truth of what had happened to his friend. After his graduation he found a good job working for one of the leading companies in the City. He remembered going through hours of security interviews and medical tests just to secure the job. The world has gone mad he thought to himself. The riots had resulted in the government slaughtering its own people that lead to out sourcing of security and protection services to a new security company responsible for protecting the people which had stringent vetting procedures. They had to collect a lot of background information about everyone especially the fact that he was linked to Frank made things worse for him. He had been one of the forefront campaigners, his face was all over the newspapers and in the news. He had been refused work before because of his links to his best friend Frank. One of the conditions of employment in the City was that he was to agree to certain rules and go for a medical. The job paid well this was a big company, so he agreed. One afternoon he was having a lunch break in the City when he bumped into Juliet. They had kept in contact soon after Frank's death they regularly met to try to resolve the issue. But for the last six months since Brian got his new job they had not spoken together.

"How has things been and how is life?" asked Brian hugging Juliet.

They hugged for a long time before she replied. She felt emotional, seeing Brian reminded her of Frank. She remembered that Friday afternoon how she had looked forward starting happiness with Frank only to be robbed. She couldn't control her tears. To her it was like yesterday, she could still picture Frank she remembered how happy he made her that first day they met. She had felt like she had known Frank all her life. Since his death she couldn't move on she felt partly responsible, she blamed herself, probably if she had agreed to meet earlier own with Frank he could still be alive. If she hadn't been jealous and suspecting Frank of maybe seeing another woman probably, she could have saved him.

"Life been okay, it is work, work for me, what about you? It has been six months since we last spoke," said Brian looking at Juliet.

She looked fabulous, he knew why Frank had been crazy about her. She was a very beautiful lady, and he felt sorry for her.

"Oh, been that long huh?" replied Juliet before she continued.

"So how is the new job, congratulations," they spoke about the new job and life in general before switching to talk about Frank.

This was a sensitive subject they both felt guilty somehow about his death. They had not been able to find any answers, and it was two years since he died. Up to now there were not any leads. Brian had been married to his university girlfriend Melissa. After Frank's death they had been very close together. His death had somehow instilled fear and a sense of realization that life is too short. He had loved his wife even more, and she was pregnant. Juliet had not thought of dating anyone after Frank's death. They talked about the riots that followed Frank's death and how this had made everything complicated.

"Hey if you want you can apply for a job here, I think the place if very good and their package is very good as well," remarked Brian as they sat down having lunch in the City.

The day was beautiful it was sunny and lovely. They were both happy to have met, this had brought up a lot of memories.

"The only drawback is the vetting procedures and you have to go for a medical which I myself think it's unnecessary," explained Brian looking at Juliet.

She paused for a little while as she couldn't stop thinking how wonderful life would have been if Frank was there together with them.

"If they pay me three times what I'm getting now, maybe I might think about it," she joked with Brian.

They spoke for some time and Brian explained that

he was getting more than he should be getting, more than the general market.

"How is that possible?" asked Juliet.

They spoke for a while and Brian explained to Juliet why he thought they paid him that money. They spoke for some time and agreed to meet soon before they headed their own way.

CHAPTER TWENTY FOUR

Since the death of Frank, Calvin had found it hard to believe the story surrounding his death, to him it was like a loss of a brother. Frank had looked at him like a brother, he felt he was a brother he had never had. He had vowed to get answers as well. But things had changed, the riots meant tight security checks and vetting. Those associated with Frank had found it hard to secure employment especially considering that they were the ones blamed for the riots that followed. To secure a job everyone had to go for tight security checks and a medical check this was the new requirement. Without this the new company responsible for security and protection would deny you employment. Calvin had refused going through such checks following the death of his friend, he had suspected that something had gone wrong and the government was responsible. After the two years without a job him being a lonely child had meant hardship for him. Both his parents were dead, they were involved in a car crash. He had been an alcoholic and had come in conflict with the government forces after Frank's death. The new security and protection company had offered him a job on condition that he undergo the medical, but he had vehemently refused. He had accused them of trying to kill him which was quickly rebuked because he was an alcoholic JT's power had grown enormously this is due to his dominating every aspect of life and taking security and protection from the government which meant in turn demanding everyone to undergo a medical as part of his condition for employment. Almost three quarters of the population worked for JT directly or indirectly. This was his dream coming true. Every day he acquired a new business, a new service and controlled most of the day-to-day services. He owned television stations, internet services, a satellite station, he had funded almost all hospital, research centers, universities, he had companies making weapons, providing military services you name it. After taking over from the government he had been a leader and an entrepreneur. He had done his best to clean his acts at least they thought. He knew now was time to build his reputation, he brought about new advances in medicines. They were miracle babies everywhere, diseases were being eradicated, and the wounded were now healing faster. Everyone associated him with longevity and prosperity. He was a family man he had his wife and daughter and commanded the respect of everyone. All this was beneficial to his plans. His aim was to dominate and rule mankind. To have a central command, to rule the whole world. Everyone who worked for him had undergone tight security vetting and a medical.

"How are you Sir?" asked the professor as she enters JT's office.

For a moment JT was silent wondering what the professor wanted.

"I'm okay and you?" he paused a little putting out his cigar. He continued.

"What brings you here, Professor, is everything okay?" he asked the professor going to his desk.

"Sit down professor," he continued before giving the professor chance to reply.

He sat on his chair and put both his legs on the table with both his hands together. There was a moment of silence, the professor was very happy she wanted to see the look on JT's face. She leaned forward.

"Sir, I now know why our subjects were failing, the project is still achievable. I figured out why we were failing," she paused a bit before continuing.

"The answer is in the ability to lower down the temperatures after the reaction. See Sir, we were not doing it right... Now I know where we were going wrong," She didn't stop she was excited delivering the news.

For some time, JT remained silent. He was relieved at least to hear this, he had expected blackmail from the professor. He felt he had made the right decision closing the project. Had the professor known that the reason for closure was the breakthrough achieved years ago then she would not have come. He remembered the first-time he met her she was equally excited about the project, but he also remembered the arguments they had about human testing. This time he had a lot to lose, he was the head of security and protection and owned a lot of businesses and service industries. He was not prepared to take any risks. He had invested a lot, and everything was going according to plan. In the past he had looked at the professor as his own daughter but this time he had a lot to lose he would rather strangle his own daughter to maintain his reputation let alone the professor. He also remembered that he had paid her tenfold the current market, most to gain her trust and cooperation but the professor had misunderstood this. What if she misunderstands again, was he prepared to take any risks? It was not until after maybe ten minutes of the professor talking that JT decided to interrupt or get involved in a conversation with her. Honestly, he didn't want anything to do with her, she knew a lot, she couldn't keep her mouth shut last time. How was he going to deal with her? These are the questions and ideas that were going through JT's head.

"What do you need professor?" asked JT putting his legs down and leaning forward.

"I want to work for you Sir, just like the old days, I want my project back, this time we will make it, I promise...," she tried her best to convince JT that she really wanted the project back.

JT's hands were tied as far as he was concerned. He was not to risk everything now in fact he did not need the professor. He had his underground team, and it was only a matter of time before things gets out of hand. Even if he offered her a job she was bound to refuse going for the medical especially spending those years experimenting on the baboons in the lab. JT had new rules he had lost half of his underground team because they had refused to undergo the medical. Those who left had seen this as a surrendering of their freedom and rights to JT. Who knows what JT was up to? Someone with that kind of wealth and power is bound to do anything in the future. The few who remained insisted on signing affidavits confirming their freedom and rights on top of generous pay packages. The professor refused human testing just a few years ago, surely, she was going to deny going through a medical knowing that she would be like the baboon in the lab.

"A lot had changed since you left," explained JT, as he stood up and took his cigar and walked to the oval glass door before opening a small window.

He puffed his cigar and for a while there was silence. The professor sat down quietly for a while before she starts talking.

"I know Sir. I was locked outside for hours Sir," JT looked at her and replied.

"See the world has changed since the riots, security and protection comes first, look now I am responsible for the protection and security of billions of people," he paused and walked towards the professor.

He sat on the corner of the table and puffed his cigar. The smoke rises in the air and the smoke seem to cover the professor's face. He apologized to the professor. He explained that nowadays things had changed. The requirements of the job or working for him meant that she had to go for a security vetting and a medical. To his surprise she agreed to undergo the medical. This gave him the assurance that somehow, she would be on his side and cooperate or, so he thought, so he offered her a job.

The doctors and nurses at the hospital where the miracle boy had rose from the dead were surprised and couldn't believe what they were witnessing. After he woke up the boy spent some days in the hospital before being sent for adoption and the doctor responsible kept in touch with the family. The first incident occurred three months after he was brought to the hospital and after three months the doctor concerned made arrangements to bring the baby to the hospital to monitor him. One night the boy woke up and escaped from the hospital and there were reports of sightings of a young boy at night running at high speed.

CHAPTER TWENTY FIVE

Juliet heard her phone ringing, and she picked it up to answer it.

"Hello Juliet, speaking," she paused and waited to hear the other person at the other end to speak.

"Yes, it's Brian, how have you been, I just phoned you to find out how things had been for you lately," replied Brian.

"Not bad and yourself?" she asked Brian.

"Been great, work is great too, but this morning," he didn't finish talking before Juliet interrupted.

"Listen about that job offer were you serious about that? Do you think I have the chance to get that job? I was thinking to change my job lately?" Juliet didn't give Brian any chance to answer his questions.

After she finished talking, there was a moment of silence both waited for each to talk. It was not until after some time that Brian replied.

"Oh yes we can organize lunch to meet my boss and we can talk over lunch I think he will agree," replied

Brian waiting for Juliet to reply.

"Oh, that's great," she replied before Brian interrupted.

"Like I said the only thing is that," he paused for a minute before continuing.

"You have to undergo a vetting procedure. That includes a medical. Most people refuse to undergo this, but I myself I agreed especially considering my background at the university and those riots, after Frank died, I had no option."

"Ok tell me more when we meet for lunch, ok?" she told Brian.

There was a moment of silence again, Brian was trying to think about the reason why he had called Juliet before he continued.

"Oh yes sure. But I called you to let you know that Calvin, you know Calvin?", Brian asked and paused.

"Oh yes, you mean Frank's friend at university, oh yes we met at the funeral," she replied.

Once she said funeral Brian paused for a while before resuming.

"He was found dead today one of my old friends at the university just rung me this morning," there was silence.

Juliet paused for a while as she remembered that day Brian told her about Frank's death. On the other side Brian heard her pulling back watery mucus from her nose before talking.

"It's a shame I couldn't believe it myself, although his death is not suspicious," he paused and gave Juliet chance to say something.

"It's still hard I remembered that night you told me about Frank," she paused before continuing.

"I don't think I will be able to forget about that day,"

there was silence as Brian also remembered that day. He remembered the look on Juliet's face as he told her about Frank's death. They spoke for some time before hanging up. Calvin was found in his room, he had hanged himself, and his landlord confirmed that he was an alcoholic, and both his parents had recently died one after the other. This was probably unbearable to him. Weeks passed by and one afternoon Juliet met with Brian to discuss the new job that was going on at his company. The pay package was three to ten times better than the current market, there was a vetting procedure involved and a medical that was to be undergone to secure the job. Once they are satisfied that you had a clean record then they would offer you employment. Brian explained that it made sense in the light of the riots that followed and the deaths of hundreds of protesters that most companies were tightening security. Brian himself had undergone the process. He explained everything involved although he was hazy about the medical. He just remembered that it lasted around 30mins, and as they explained a small hole was to be drilled and a sample of his blood or marrow was taken. No pain or anything afterwards. You can opt for anesthetic or not your choice. After all this then you get a job. She agreed to do her own research first about the company before undergoing this and taking the job. By this time JT controlled billions of people all over the continent. Most governments acquired JT's services to help protect their own people. He was a global phenomenon. After the riots people in other countries had started not trusting their governments. A third-party like a private company was to be responsible for the protection of the people.

Governments had gone mad that they become so oppressive that people's freedom and rights were often abused. These governments were killing their own people. The world was changing. Third parties were like intermediaries, they had power to protect the people, and they were answerable to both the government and the people to some extent. JT as the head of security and protection had insisted that for everyone to be protected they had to undergo the medical procedure. All people in the government had undergone the medical procedure apart from the few who were suspicious that in case there will be an abuse of power by JT himself then who will hold JT to account. One of the people who had quit the government was a young man called Patrick. Patrick was in his early thirties he had been suspicious of everyone that at times his friends had thought that he was nuts. After the riots and slaughter of many and the taking of protection and security by the private company Patrick had refused to go for the vetting and medical procedure and instead chose to quit and start his own business. Years down the line he had found it hard to keep his company open, JT controlled everything and did not deal with anyone who was not part of his security and protection system. He had refused anything to do with this. He refused on personal reasons the government had slaughtered many during the days of the riots what if this private company was going to slaughter even? more maybe thousands. It was not long after the professor had agreed to go for vetting and medical that she bumped into Patrick. Patrick at this time was struggling, he had no business or money. He found it hard to associate with others as most of them were in the security system. Dealing with those who had no any links with those in the program was seen as jeopardizing the system and therefore forbidden. Out of sympathy or so it seems she had agreed to help Patrick with money and food. She tried to convince him to join the security and protection program, but he refused. It was not long before things start going off hand as JT saw it. Patrick's feelings for the professor grew fast that they spent more time together. The professor merely saw Patrick as a friend she was there to help him so that maybe one day he might agree to help her with her research. JT knew either way there could be troubled in the future. Patrick had vehemently refused to join his program, in fact Patrick was opposed to the whole idea. This was risky he was not willing to take any chances. Any bad publicist would be catastrophic and would jeopardize his work. The following days he made sure that the professor spent more time in the lab, working hard and sleeping a few hours. The next day he called her to his office.

"Professor I understand you have been very busy and I am very grateful for that," he paused for a while before continuing.

"I need you to work over the weekend as well if you can," explained JT and waited for her response.

She had worked the whole week sleeping just a few hours in the lab and to add weekend as well was unbearable. She thought for some time, she was planning to sleep the whole weekend. JT realized that she was not going to agree, so he offered incentives.

"If you do this for me," he paused before continuing.

"I will not only double your salary this month, but you can have some days off next week," as she heard this, she agreed to work the weekend as well. JT before he left stood there for some time looked at her smiled and left.

CHAPTER TWENTY SIX

The city is dark, the skies are filled with black smoke from burning cars and buildings. There are riots in the city and crowds are gathering in large numbers. You can hear helicopters hovering in the sky and at very low heights. You can hear shouting and screaming from a distance. There are men and women marching towards the city shouting and holding banners and some holding weapons in the form of sticks and stones. From every corner you can see groups of people shouting and all marching towards the center of the city. The city is in chaos you can hear all kinds of noises from every corner of the city and the noise of the helicopters hovering above.

"We want answers!" shouted one of the people leading the crowds towards the city.

"Yes, today we want an end to all this," responded the crowd in a loud simultaneous voice and you can hear echoes from the sky scrapers lining the major road to the city.

"How many more!" shouted the leader of the group

facing the following crowd.

For a moment the marching crowd stood still, and silence broke out for a few seconds as the leader of the group jumped on top of the nearby auto machine to address the crowd. All you can hear from a distance is the noise of the hovering flying machines above and the sound of the burning glass, cars and buildings.

"We want answers!" the crowd shouted in one voice.

"We want an end to all this," added the crowd with some in the crowd raising the weapons which they were carrying and some raising their fists.

"How many more! I ask you, how many more is enough!" shouted the leader of the group this time with a raised voice at the same time punching the air with his clenched fist.

"It has to end today!" shouted one of the members of the leading group jumping on top of the parked cars on the other side of the road.

You can hear the clapping of hands and shouting as in agreement within the crowd and others whistling and jumping up and down raising their weapons. With one voice the crowd shouted.

"It ends today!".

You can hear roars, chanting and the ground vibrating to the jumping up and down of the crowd. Some members of the crowd who were on the edges of the group started smashing windows of cars and the glass of offices and shops nearby. The crowd started marching forward singing, chanting and roaring raising weapons up and down breaking anything in their way marching towards the center of the city. As soon as they started advancing towards the city the flying machines can be heard approaching swiftly, you can hear the hovering noise as they approach the forwarding crowd. There is noise from every corner of the city. As they approach the center of the city, a large building can be seen tightly secured with large fences and metal steel gates and with several guards holding weapons. From a distance the building is so huge and tall that it seems to touch the sky and it is surrounded by large water ponds. You can see flying machines hovering above it and large flashing lights which seem to reflect all the way to the top of the sky. The sky above it is dark, filled with smoke of burning buildings and cars. A large rotating flashing beacon can be seen circling the grounds in front of the building. As the crowd approached, the big metal gates started closing slowing. Just in front of the crowd a metal barricade seems to appear from nowhere blocking the crowd and holding them back from the grounds in front of the large fence and metal steel gates. This caused some panic as for a moment some people started running backwards before a large voice shouted.

"Fear not! Let's stand our ground! We are not afraid. How many more should die! How many more I ask you?"

Those who had panicked as soon as the metal barricade appeared in front of them gathered their courage and started moving forward close to their leader. The leader stood just behind the barricade facing the crowd. There were roars, chanting and singing among the crowd. The whole group started jumping up and down. Some jumping on top of the automobiles smashing glasses and windows. Others started throwing whatever they can towards the big building shouting and chanting.

"How many more! How many more! How many more should die! It has to end today!" repeated the crowd as they jumped up and down raising their weapons and throwing stones, bottles and metal things towards the big building.

The ground vibrated in response to the jumping up and down of the crowd. The flying machines started hovering at low heights circulating the crowd. A few people among the crowd can be seen taking cover, some retreating and some hiding behind parked cars. Big flashing lights can be seen cutting through the crowds as the flying machines hover above the crowd. The lights mainly focused on the leading group just behind the high metal barriers protecting the ground in front of the main fence to the buildings. People had gathered in the city demanding answers and an end to the killings of future leaders. A big crowd had gathered at the headquarters of the city. The people were very angry and were ready to start a fight. The headquarters were securely protected; metal steel barriers had rose from the ground stopping the crowd reaching the grounds of the headquarters. Flying machines were hovering above, extra city security protectors had been deployed to deal with any riots. A big screen in front of the city was switched on and after some time a big man appeared on the screen trying to address the crowd. The crowd refused to listen, they started shouting that they cannot talk to a screen they demanded the man to appear in person in front of them. The crowd started singing and throwing whatever they can at the big screen and a mash fence suddenly appeared in front of the screen. They got angrier and kept singing and marching. A large voice can be heard on the big speakers attached to the headquarters building. The voice is demanding the crowd to be quiet and listen or otherwise removed from the grounds by force. No one seemed to listen, the people got aggressive, singing and chanting whilst jumping up and down. That goes for a while until the man re appeared on the big screen again.

"Silence, listen to me," shouted the man on the screen.

"If you have queries please formally submit these in a peaceful manner and we will do our best to address these in due time," continued the man.

"Silence, listen please go back to your homes," the man disappeared from the big screen for some time.

No one gave noticed as the leader of the group started addressing the crowd mid-way through the speech.

"Today is the day we stand our ground, we can't be intimidated and threatened. Tell me if the dead were alive today, what will say?" he paused, paced from left to right and back looking at those who were in front straight into their eyes.

"Today we need an answer! Today we need an end to this," he clenched his fist and punched the air.

The crowd responded and shouted, others clapping hands and others chanting slogans. The man reappeared on the big screen and this time warned the crowd that the headquarters of the city will be defended at any cost so, they should take his warning seriously and march back to their homes or else they will be removed by force and a curfew imposed.

"We are not afraid, we fight to the end, we never give up, we never surrender our freedom and rights," screamed the crowd.

The ground vibrated to the jumping up and down of the crowd who continued smashing glasses and windows of shops, offices and cars. Others at the fringes set cars on fire. Black smoke filled the skies of the city. Big military trucks like firefighting trucks surrounded the crowds. The man reappeared on the screen this time with what he referred to as the last warning. He ordered the crowd to disperse immediately or be forced to, suddenly the trucks pointed huge pipes towards the crowds, few people started panicking and taking cover. Suddenly flashing amber lights on top of the fence poles turned on and a siren can be heard getting louder and louder. The crowd raised their voices as well, jumping up and down. A number 30 appeared on the big screen and suddenly the flashing amber lights turned into a red and a voice can be heard telling everyone that this is their last warning and to disperse immediately or be forced to. They all suddenly started throwing whatever they can at the trucks. The crowd in front did not move at all but become more and more aggressive, then the countdown begun. 29, 28, 27, 26........

"We won't be intimidated we fight today!" shouted the crowd knowing they were going to be attacked.

The leader gave gestures to all the people preparing them for an attack trying to avoid causalities. 10, 9, 8, 7, 6....... they knew this was it the fight had begun. Before they knew it, the pipes released pressurized water that knocked some to the ground, but those who had listened and understood the leader's gestures and ducked lying on the ground avoiding being hit by the pressurized water. Some took cover behind parked cars and others ran backwards. That went on for some time and the big man appeared again on the screen and warned them to disperse immediately. Another countdown started immediately as the man disappeared from the big screen, 30,29, 28.... The protectors of the headquarters started forming two straight lines from left to right and marching forward shouting all in one voice. They marched holding butt sticks and stood behind the fence that had appeared from nowhere, they stood there marching raising their knees to their chest levels. The crowd anticipated what was going to happen and prepared for battle, suddenly the fence in front of them suddenly disappeared underground and the battle began. The fight went on for some time and the crowd seemed to be winning until reinforcements marched forward and started slowly pushing the crowd backwards. The leader shouted some words, and the crowd seemed to run away backwards which made the city protectors chase after them only to be ambushed as those fleeing ran either to the left or right side introducing those fresh at the back to face the approaching city protectors. The city protectors seemed to target those whom they thought had much influence and in groups they attack them leaving them for dead. In some way this helped the crowd as they started pushing them backwards. The city protectors tried to do the same tactic, but the leader of the crowd had anticipated this beforehand and shouted to the crowd to stand their ground as he had seen the reinforcements being deployed. The city protectors formed a line and marched back to the headquarters in a line. Those who had been injured limped back as well, the other city protectors picked up their injured members and marched backwards as well.

CHAPTER TWENTY SEVEN

The crowd started shouting and chanting even more.
"We won't be bullied, we won't be intimidated, we fight today," others started clapping hands and throwing weapons at them.
The big man appeared on the screen, he didn't say anything for some time, it appeared that he was looking at the crowd, he looked sideways of the screen and a new set of city protectors appeared with guns. Flying machines started hovering on top of the crowds. Flashing red lights were switched on and the new set of city protectors took positions holding rifles in front of the defeated city protectors. Another countdown began 30, 29, 28, 27, suddenly, the hovering flying machines released bomb shells into the crowd, there was white smoke everywhere, and the crowd started coughing and falling to the ground others running for their lives. The area was filled with smoke and gun shots were heard that sends everyone into panic and taking cover. Suddenly, the area in

front of the building was empty with a few injured still lying down. Another set of bullets noise can be heard that sends the crowd running backwards and made them take cover. After a while the smoke disappeared but the flying machines kept hovering above. The crowd realized that the bullets had been fired into the skies and there were no causalities, they gathered some distance behind and started chanting and shouting. That went on for some time before a gunshot can be heard that sends the whole crowd running for cover. No one seemed to have seen who fired it and everyone took cover. They lay on the ground for some time taking cover in case they are shot at again. A few minutes passed whilst still on the floor, their leader shouted some words, and they got up on their feet again. They stood for a moment waiting to see what had happened. On the other end a few city protectors left their positions and rushed towards one of them who seemed to be lying on the ground. They surrounded him, and he had both his hands on his neck. Blood was gushing out of his neck some from the mouth and nose. They fought to save him, but he kept bleeding and stopped moving after a few minutes. One of the city protectors marched to his leader who was standing behind at the back near the headquarters entrance and said something in his ear. Suddenly, he pulled out his pistol and fired a shot in the skies. The city protectors who had rifles marched forward and aimed their rifles at the crowds. Everyone knew this was war now they started taking cover at the advice of their leader. Shots were fired into the crowd and some lay dead and some crawled with bullet wounds away from the scene.

CHAPTER TWENTY EIGHT

Tanya had investigated the deaths of former activists and former government security forces, they had all died in mysterious ways. For most they had suffered some form of high temperatures and trauma. Brian's death, at first seemed more of an accident than anything else. It was only after she received leaked documents of his autopsy that she realized that there was more to it than meets the eye. His body had been cooked when he was still alive and despite his car plunging in the water where he died that did not help to cool his body either. It seemed he had been cooked from the inside out. Although his death looked like an accident, the state of his body pointed to something more sinister. It seemed he suffered some high temperatures and his organs stopped working when he was alive. He might have lost unconsciousness whilst driving which led to his car plunging into the river. His leaked file also indicated that he had undergone a medical with JT's security and protection establishment. He was still employed by one of JT's companies in the city. Tanya went to Brian's company to investigate his death but was refused entry as she was not part of the security and protection program. She researched more about Brian and found out his home address and information that he was married to a one, Melissa. At Brian's house the door was left unlocked and after a few knocks on the door, she entered inside as no one had answered. She found out that Brian that morning had raised suspicion to the whereabouts of his friend who was to start work at his company that morning. He had asked his wife to meet him, at this other lady's house. She listened to the message left on the answer phone again and again. The picture that was now clear to her was that Brian, had been worried about his friend, who apparently did not turn up for work. In hearing this and trying to contact this other lady to no avail, he decided to go to her house and asked his wife to meet her there. Tanya did not know the other lady, she tried to get the information from Brian's company in the city but was denied access to any files or privileged information. Brian had been at the university with his wife but there was no information about the other lady mentioned in the left message on the answer phone. After days of researching Tanya finally found the other lady's address. She drove to her house, and on arrival she noticed that there were two cars in the drive way. After running a vehicle registration check she later found out that the cars belonged to a one Melissa and a one Juliet. She entered the house and found two bodies presumably Melissa and Juliet. They were all in a bad state, Juliet had died first possibly days before Melissa discovered her body. Melissa probably slipped and fell hitting her head on the corner of the tube which caused her to lose a lot of blood. This could be her cause of death, it all looked accidental. She went through Juliet's stuff to try to get more information but with little success. There were messages on the answer phone left by Brian and her friends congratulating her about the new job. Before she could investigate the place furthermore she was shown out by the security and protection establishment who had appeared from nowhere quarantining the place for investigations. Later that day she had heard that two other people had been found dead as well in a different city. What interested her more about this was that the other lady who had died was still working for JT. Although her death was not suspicious, it seems there was a burglary, and the intruder strangled and drowned her before getting shot in the head by the security forces. She visited the area later that day. This time she was not denied access to her surprise as the security and protection services were already there. JT had insisted that the place be left alone, it was best if someone else had discovered the bodies. He was not afraid, he had planned this carefully, that in the end anyone would conclude that they were all accidental deaths. After clearing out all his enemies JT saw him as invincible. Surely no one was to stand in his way, he had accumulated a lot of power and control. In the months that followed, JT kept taking out all his enemies. He had declared cleaning up of all those against what he stood for. All those who refused to join his security and protection system soon found themselves marginalized, without jobs or any sayings to things that matter to them. She went inside and took notes and investigated the place. The body was in a bad state as well; she had drowned taking a bath possibly strangled first by the intruder. She later discovered that the intruder was the homeless Victor. On further investigations it appeared that this homeless guy had broken into the apartment before and was apprehended only to be released after being cautioned and banned from going to that apartment again. It was the neighbors who raised the alarm after hearing the commotion. The security forces were quick to respond, and he was shot as soon as he left the apartment. In her investigations she found out that all of them had links to the activist groups and to those who had rioted a few years back. They were also linked to the murdered activist Frank. Was all this a coincident or there was something more sinister about all this? JT was a highly protected man, he had body guards all the time, no one, who was not in his security and protection program was allowed near him. He was invincible, the only man who had laid hands on JT was TK, Clara's boyfriend the musician, but that was a long time ago. JT had spared his life only because of Clara. JT was hard to target; he was a loyal man, a man of principles in the eyes of many, but the devil himself to the very few who had experienced his wrath. Tanya had realized that the only way to end all this was to take out the man himself, but that was impossible considering the current circumstances. Sleepless nights after sleepless nights Tanya had tried to find a way of infiltrating JT's circles. She had remembered all those years in the regiment, and all her training and teachings. But she couldn't find a way to terminate JT, it seems the man was three times ahead of her. He was fortified and would not deal with anyone not in his program.

CHAPTER TWENTY NINE

One evening she received a phone call from a man who wanted her services. The man left no name but arranged to meet her in one of the coffee bars in the city. At first, she did not attend the meeting, she knew this could be a setup. Having read a lot of stories about JT, she sensed that she might be on JT's hit list. Knowing the man JT was, she was scared he might take her out anytime. JT never hesitated, any threat real or perceived, he would act on it in a flash. Over the following weeks TK was found shot in the head several times. There were a lot of stories surrounding his death. At first it was claimed that one of the boyfriend of the ladies he bedded had got him killed. TK was a womanizer, him being a musician meant crossing boundaries and changing women like he did socks. In every city he traveled, he had a mistress or so. At one-point he had gone out with his girlfriend's best friend.

Tanya knew somehow there was more to it than what

she heard. Having learnt that TK had a confrontational with JT at one-point, she knew that JT was somehow involved in his death. She knew the day TK punched JT was the day he technically died it was only a matter of time for JT had signed his death certificate on that day. She set up to investigate TK's death. After seeing TK's crime scene photos and how he was shot, she knew that whoever shot him had some military training. He had a three-point shoot to kill mark common among military personnel especially those guarding high-ranking officials and presidents. Clara didn't want to grieve much for her boyfriend, TK, who had become a pain to her and their daughter. She remembered all those lonely nights and all those nights he came back home in the middle of the night drunk and disorderly. And all those beatings and abuse she suffered at his hands. She remembered how he went out with her best friend that was the final act. She had sometimes wished that he was dead. Nevertheless, he was still the father of their daughter, and when he died, she took some time off work. She had worked for JT for many years and had taken few weeks going on holidays. She is one of the people JT trusted, they had spent numerous times together. JT had insisted that she come back to work after a few days of mourning, but she had insisted on taking more weeks instead as she insisted on spending more time with her daughter. One afternoon Tanya picked up the phone and called one of her old-time friends. They had been in the presidential guards together, but she was now working undercover as a secretary. She insisted that she wanted her help, and they arranged to meet as they could not talk over the phone. The couple of weeks that followed, they met regularly to discuss a lot of issues. Tanya saw her as the perfect person she wanted to infiltrate JT's security and protection program. They met in private and they draw up plans. It was such a good time for them being together as they remembered all those years in the regiment some years back. Over the coming weeks they had put a detailed plan in place and it was not long before Tanya's friend was working for JT. She had temporarily replaced Clara who took more time off work following the death of TK. Naomi had been vetted and had agreed to undergo a medical which she passed. Over the coming weeks she had passed information to Tanya about JT's habits. This was the information she wanted to understand the man and come up with a plan. Over the coming weeks Clara could not cope with the death of TK. She thought she had moved on, but she wasn't prepared to go back to work anytime sooner, JT still paid her salary in full. She had realized how important life was and wanted to spend more time with her daughter. This was a bonus to Tanya's plan. One morning everything seemed ok, and it was business as usual. Naomi JT's new secretary didn't turn up for work. At last moment JT scrambled his PR to cover for the new secretary. He didn't want to replace her so early. She didn't even make a phone call to let JT know why she was not at work. The following day she was back at work, she had told JT that she had an abusive boyfriend who had attacked her the previous night. She had bruising on her face and had insisted that she was shy to come to work as the bruising was worse the previous day. The same happened again two or three times over the next weeks and JT insisted that the PR cover for the new secretary. This was a blow to Tanya's plans as she had hoped that JT would scramble another secretary at short notice. It seemed her plan had failed as a few days later Clara came back to work for JT and the new secretary left. The only good thing was that she now had inside information about JT. She had learnt a lot and one day she would be lucky, and that day she would take her chances and rewrite history, she thought to herself. Months had passed by and one afternoon, Tanya received a phone call from her friend Naomi.

"This is it, this is the moment you were waiting for, take your chances soldier," the phone line soon died.

Tanya had been waiting for this day since she learnt that JT was behind the murder of all those people including her father. Her father had been assassinated months after she opened the investigating company. This had not discouraged her or stopped her from trying to find the truth. Somehow, she felt the need to revenge her father's death. She spent hours that night of the phone call, doing her makeup and preparing for the following day. She had rehearsed everything repeatedly. She had a few hours' sleep before she headed to the big city. For most it seemed like an everyday morning, everyone running about minding their own business. It was a chilly morning, Tanya couldn't stop thinking about those years in the regiment, all her training, and how her dream was shattered when the security and protection establishment took over from the government. Her father's death made her feel like crying. Her father had been shot in the head at point blank. She pulled over on the side of the road for some time gathering her nerves. She unplugged her electric cigarette and waited for few minutes on the road side puffing.

CHAPTER THIRTY

JT had just arrived at work, it was another day at the
office as usual. The only difference was that Clara was
not there the time he arrived for work. She normally
started work early, and her knowing JT, she knew he
wanted to come to work and find her already there.
He went straight into his office and sat on his desk.
He checked his diary, and it seemed he was busier
that day than any other days. He had appointments
the whole day but later in the day. The morning was
quiet than usual. This was due to the phone call he
received late the previous night. JT sat in his office
checking his schedule for the day, he had a busy day
ahead of him he thought to himself. Tanya had waited
for this day for a very long time. She arrived at the
building, she had never felt like this before, she was
very nervous. It was early in the morning, but she
could feel the sweat on her palms and forehead. She
stood at the entrance for a while her heart beating so
fast. She gathered her nerves, took out the swipe card

and waited for a while. She took a long breath and wiped her palms on her short dress and moved close to the scanning machine. This is it, she thought to herself. She waited for a short while and then swiped the card.

"Beep, beep," she heard a beeping sound that sends a cold shiver through her spine.

She took the swipe card and rubbed it on her dress before trying again. This time she heard a long continuous sound before the door in front of her started opening. She took another long breath and entered the building. As soon as she entered the building, she saw another door in front of her. She was asked to place her palm on the screen or to enter her access code. She whispered to herself before typing on the keyboard.

"Access granted."

She heard a female voice coming out from the speakers next to the scanning machine. The reception was a very big room with some sofas against the wall next to a large door. This could be JT's office, she thought to herself. JT was in his office preparing for a busy day ahead of him when he heard a knock on the door. He didn't answer straight away he waited for another knock. After some seconds had passed, he heard another knock on the door and this time he answered.

"Come in," he said with a raised voice.

The door slowly opened, and he sat up straight in his chair with both his hands on the table as if he was trying to stand up. A lady came in, Naomi, he thought to himself looking in his diary in front of him. Tanya walked in and stood in the middle of the office. She looked at JT who was scrolling his diary with his face looking down.

"It's going to be a very busy day," remarked JT before raising his head to look at Naomi. She didn't say anything but stood there for a while. JT sat back in his chair, looked at Naomi. For some time, there was a moment of silence. Suddenly, he realized that something was not right as Naomi stood there in front of him. It all happened very fast, but JT knew there was something wrong. He tried to distract Naomi.

"Cigar," he asked Naomi who was standing in front of him.

"No thank you," she replied with a low voice putting her hands on her sides.

JT looked down, opened his drawer and withdrew a small box which he placed on the table. Tanya's heart started beating very fast, she looked at the small box and waited for JT's next move. JT opened the small box and took out a cigar. He clearly had Naomi's image in his head and he knew there was something wrong with the lady in front of her, but just couldn't tell what. He put the cigar in his mouth, looked at Naomi and waited for a while. It was just a few minutes since Tanya had entered JT's office but to her it seemed like a long time. She realized that she had to make the first move before JT tried to do something foolish. Tanya saw JT put his left-hand underneath the table and his right hand in his drawer as if reaching for something. Quickly she pulled her short dress upwards revealing her black knickers that seemed to distract JT for a while. She pulled out a gun from one of her thighs and aimed at JT. JT's left-hand was on the button underneath his desk and his right hand was already in the drawer. Tanya thought JT was reaching for a lighter as he had his cigar in his mouth. It all happened very fast, in a fraction of a second, she saw JT pulling a gun from his drawer and in a panic, she fired a shot at JT. He pulled out his gun and shot Tanya before holding his neck with his left-hand. Tanya staggered backwards and fired two more shots at JT before falling to the ground. She crawled towards the door before seeing the door being opened. She rolled sideways and fired a shot at JT's bodyguard who entered the office, hitting him in the head. She got up and staggered towards the door holding her chest. She pulled the heavy door open, peeped outside and staggered outside. She ran a few steps and looked backwards, but no one was following. She staggered away from JT's office building and as she staggered away, she remembered a time when she was a little girl playing with her father. She remembered running fast to her dad, who in turn lifted her up. She remembered the smile on his face and how happy she was. She remembered stretching her arms and flying like a bird as he lifted her up. Just a few more steps, a car suddenly pulled up in front of her.

"Quick, quick, get in!"

The passenger door opened as the car suddenly came to a halt and as she jumped into the car, the car sped off.

Elina Salajeva

THE END

Elina Salajeva

9 781916 439740